'We had two new girls that second term, but poor old Mouse hardly got noticed because the other girl was the nearly-famous Araminta Eversage, star of stage, screen and cat food advertisement. She drove Mrs Mackie nearly round the bend, caused a fight between Cerise, even sillier this term, and Philippa. But then she also revolutionised our lives . . .'

Mickey Young
First Year
Park Wood Girls' School

Also by Mary Hooper

Short Cut to Love
Making Waves
Lexie
Cassie
Janey's Diary
Janey's Summer
School Friends 1: First Term

MARY HOOPER

School Friends 2

STAR

MAMMOTH

First published in Great Britain 1991
by Mammoth, an imprint of Mandarin Paperbacks
Michelin House, 81 Fulham Road, London SW3 6RB

Mandarin is an imprint of the Octopus Publishing Group

Text copyright © 1991 Mary Hooper

A CIP catalogue record for this title
is available for the British Library

ISBN 0 7497 0296 6

Printed in Great Britain
by Cox & Wyman Ltd

Contents

Chapter One
ENTER THE STAR!

Sitting on the school bus and going towards Park Wood Girls' on the first day of the Spring term I felt very different from that day last September when I first went to Park Wood.

Everyone on the bus looked quite pleased to be back, and we all had our Christmas presents to brag or moan about so the journey went really quickly. I was looking forward to seeing my best friend, Fleur.

In fact, I was really looking forward to this term – and hoping that I wouldn't put my foot in it quite so many times. Perhaps this would be the term I'd stun everyone with my unbelievable skill at something-or-other. On the other hand, perhaps it wouldn't . . .

When we drove into the school playground, Cerise was outside waiting for the buses to arrive – Cerise in bright pink tights and fluffy earmuffs, of course! And *how* many times had Mrs Mackie, our form teacher, had a go at her about only wearing school uniform?

She waved at me excitedly and came over.

'Waiting for me?' I said.

'Silly Mickey! I wouldn't be waiting to show you into the school, would I? You know where to go.'

I patted the pink furry earmuffs. 'I see the earmuffs are on. I thought they were just for skiing?'

'Mummy says my ears are very delicate and I should protect them these cold mornings,' she said. 'Anyway, you know I like to wear something cerise because my . . .'

'I know, I know!' I said hurriedly, before she started going on about it.

She'd had us all in fits of giggles on the first day last term when she turned up in a kind of 'designer' school uniform and had a tearful goodbye with 'mummy' in the playground.

'D'you like them?' she said. 'They're real dyed rabbit fur. Aren't they gorgeous?'

I shuddered; I'd had a pet rabbit once so I hated things made out of rabbit fur.

'Suit me, don't they?' she said.

I hid a grin. With her mop of fluffy permed hair and pink earmuffs she looked like a pekingese with ear trouble.

'Did you get some good prezzies?' she asked, and then didn't wait for me to tell her but went on, 'I got a whole new beauty box full

8

of make-up – hundreds of different coloured eyeshadows!'

'What, for hundreds of different-coloured eyes?'

'Oh, *you*!' she said.

Another bus drew up and Fleur got off. I waved to her and she came over and joined us. It was really nice to see her again.

'Mummy says it's never too soon to start practising with make-up,' Cerise said when she'd told Fleur about the wonders of the new make-up box. 'I want to be a model and models have to know all about lipsticks and eyeshadows and things.'

Fleur nodded solemnly. 'Of course. It's very important.'

'Is there an exam in it?' I asked. 'GCSE in putting on mascara?'

'Oh, I should think so,' Fleur said, and Cerise looked from one of us to the other, not quite sure if we were messing around or not. 'First question: what is best for a party, mascara with little glittery bits, or mascara to match your dress?'

Cerise frowned, then pushed me. 'You're taking the mickey, aren't you?' she said, and then laughed. 'That's quite funny, isn't it – taking the mickey, Mickey!'

'Well, it might be if I hadn't heard it about four hundred times before,' I said.

'What are you hanging about here for?' Fleur asked her. 'Aren't you coming in? I want to see our new classroom.'

9

We'd heard at the end of last term that we – Mrs Mackie's class, that is – had been moved. As well as being keen to see our classroom I was also dying to see all our friends and find out what sort of a Christmas they'd had.

Cerise shook her head. 'I'm not coming in yet,' she said, 'I'm waiting for Araminta.'

'What's Araminta?' Fleur and I both asked together.

'The new girl!'

'I thought her name was Jane something?' I said.

Mrs Mackie had told us a new girl was starting this term – a girl from stage school who'd done some television parts. We'd been told that she'd had a part in *Village Life*, a soap, but no one had actually been able to work out who she was or what part she played.

'Her name's actually Jane Hutt,' Cerise went on, glad to be the bearer of this information, 'but her stage name – her professional name – is Araminta Eversage.'

'Weird!' I said.

'It sounds like a herb shampoo,' Fleur said.

'She plays Avril Smithson – the farmer's daughter in *Village Life*,' Cerise said. 'On Christmas Day she was on television delivering a calf. Didn't you see her?'

Fleur had seen her, but I hadn't. 'Who are you, then, Cerise?' Fleur asked her. 'The welcoming committee?'

'I asked Mrs Mackie if I could wait out

10

here for her,' Cerise said. 'Just so she doesn't feel lost.'

'And also to find out if she's got any signed photographs of Patrick Parker, I bet!' I added. He was the teenage star of *Village Life* and Cerise was a bit daft about him.

'D'you think she will have?' Cerise breathed with a sigh.

'Perhaps he'll come with her,' Fleur teased, 'just to see if she settles in all right on her first morning.'

'Ooh, you don't really think so, do you?' Cerise could be heard squealing as we went off.

'How did you get on in Scotland?' I asked Fleur. 'Did your gran fill you up with porridge and keep stuffing you with haggis? Doesn't look like it, you still look really slim.'

'Not *really* slim,' she said, pulling at the waist band of her navy school skirt, 'but I'm better than I was, aren't I?'

'Definitely,' I assured her. She'd been really porky last September, but then she'd gone on a sponsored slim and had ended up just chubbyish.

'Mum had to buy me a new skirt two sizes smaller,' she said. She gave a little skip. 'I'm dying to see everyone, aren't you?'

I nodded. 'Everyone except Mrs Mackie.'

'Everyone except Mrs Mackie and *Alison*,' she added.

'Mmm . . . I almost forgot her,' I said. Alison was horrible; the class bully. She was always

11

trying to push us around and had even taken to pinching things – crisps and choccy bars usually – until we'd played a trick on her.

'D'you think she'll be just as horrible this term?'

Fleur shook her head. 'She got such a shock that day we hid all that stuff in her desk I shouldn't think she'd ever dare steal anything from anyone again.'

'We'll have to watch her, though,' I said, 'especially with the new girl.'

'Will you be able to go skiing with the school at Easter, d'you think?' Fleur asked.

'Hope so,' I said longingly. I wasn't much good at sporty things – well, not much good was an understatement; when my brothers Jamie and Paul had heard I might go skiing they'd said they were going to keep a hundred miles from the French alps and put out avalanche warnings. 'How about you?' I asked Fleur.

'Dad says I can, Mum says I can't,' she said with a grin, 'but I'm working on it. Mind you,' she patted her tummy, 'I'll have to go on losing weight. Whenever I think about skiing I think of those fat people in the cartoons: they fall down and then roll over and over until they arrive at the bottom as a huge snowball with their feet sticking out.'

We went into class and hung our duffle coats in our lockers. The new classroom wasn't particularly exciting; it was smaller than our old one if anything, and the only real difference was the outlook – the other one had over-looked the playing field whereas this one had a view of the neighbouring boys' school playground.

There weren't many of our class in yet, just Philippa and Su and Alice, and they were all doing typical-for-them sorts of things. Alice had found herself a new desk down at the front and was busy setting all her stuff out in it neatly. Alice was nice but a bit of a goody-goody; her sister had been head girl and Alice never let us forget it. Su, whose parents had a Chinese takeaway in town, was sitting quietly reading a teenage magazine and Philippa, class creep, was nosing into one of the cupboards behind Mrs Mackie's desk.

Philippa asked if there was any sign of the new girl.

I shook my head. 'Cerise is heading a one-girl reception committee outside in the playground, though.' I looked round; it was unusual to see Philippa without her best friend Annabel – she'd spent the whole of last term attached to her like a shadow. 'Where's Annabel, then?' I asked.

Annabel was nice – much nicer than Philippa, actually. Her parents had pots of money and a huge house with practically a park round it and we'd thought she was really snobby at first, but she'd turned out to be all right.

'I don't know,' Philippa said anxiously. 'She wasn't on the bus this morning. I hope she's not ill or anything.'

'I hope she turns up soon,' Fleur said, 'you look quite strange not being attached to the side of anyone – as if something's missing.'

Philippa pulled a face at Fleur. 'Here, you'll never guess . . .' she said then, and Fleur and I groaned.

'Not already!' I said. 'Not a dire and dark secret *this* early in the term.'

'It's about the new girl,' Philippa went on. 'Mrs Mackie said her name was Jane Hutt, but that's just the name she was born with. Her stage name's . . .'

'Araminta Eversage!' Fleur finished.

'How did *you* know?' Philippa said, quite put out.

There was a scuffling noise outside in the corridor and then the twins could be heard: *'It's down here, I tell you!' 'No, it isn't, Mrs Mackie didn't say it was in this block!' 'Why don't you just believe me?' 'Oh, you always think you know everything, you do . . .'* and then Arina and Jasbir came through the door, arm in arm but with indignant, cross faces. They were practically identical, except that Jasbir had straight-down-the-back plaits while Arina wore her long hair in a topknot. It was useful for telling them apart.

'Told you!' Arina said triumphantly to her twin. 'I said they'd all be in here!'

'Well, Mrs Mackie must have changed her mind . . .' Jasbir said moodily, and I grinned. The holidays hadn't changed *them*, they were still rowing.

14

The classroom filled up quickly after that: Erica, Alison, Laura, Wendy and everyone piled in and everyone started talking excitedly, so it was a bit of a nuisance when Mrs Mackie came in with the register under her arm and ordered everyone to sit down and be quiet.

Mrs Mackie wasn't too bad as a form teacher, I suppose. She was grey and stern and could be highly sarcastic – especially if we didn't live up to the standards of the precious first years she'd had before us, but she could be quite funny, too.

She sorted out the few remaining girls who hadn't got themselves desks and Fleur and I settled ourselves at the back.

I craned my neck to look round the class. 'Still no sign of Annabel,' I said. 'What will Philippa do without her?'

'I bet she's gone to a private school,' Fleur said. 'I could never understand what she was doing here in the first place; her parents are so rich.'

I nodded. 'Remember the swimming pool party?'

'How could I forget!' Fleur said. Annabel had invited us to her house to have a swim in the indoor pool but then her mother had turned up and chucked us all out.

Mrs Mackie clapped her hands. 'Now, can I have some quiet, please, girls!' she said. 'I know it's the first day of term and all very exciting but we've got a lot of things to get

15

through.' She looked round at us over her old-fashioned pink-rimmed glasses, 'Now, where's the new girl?'

Philippa put up her hand. 'She's not here yet, Mrs Mackie.'

'Isn't she?' Mrs Mackie said. 'I hope that just because she's a TV star she doesn't think she can choose her own hours.'

'Excuse me,' came a little voice from near the front of the class. 'I *am* here.'

Mrs Mackie readjusted her glasses and stared at the girl who'd spoken and the rest of us craned our necks to look at her. She was small – tiny – with soft brown hair and a timid expression. I hadn't even noticed her before.

'Who are you?' Mrs Mackie asked.

'The new girl,' she whispered, looking as if she'd like to sink into the floor.

There was a stir of interest from round the class – and then a murmur of disbelief. *This* little mouse-like thing couldn't possible be the TV star we were expecting.

'Really?' Mrs Mackie asked. 'You're Jane Hutt, are you?'

'No,' the girl said, 'I'm Marie McCombie.'

We all breathed a sigh of relief; how disappointing if *she'd* turned out to be the TV star.

'The school secretary told me to come in here. You are Mrs Mackie, aren't you?'

'Well, I was the last time I looked!' Mrs Mackie said, and we all laughed dutifully at the joke we'd heard a few dozen times before. She shuffled the pieces of paper on her desk and eventually found a letter. 'Sorry,' she said, 'yes, here we are. Marie McCombie, you've come from Cornwall, haven't you?'

'That's right,' Marie said.

'Sorry,' Mrs Mackie said, 'I've got so many other pieces of paper here that the letter about you went to the bottom of the pile. Now, are you all right sitting there?'

'Yes, thank you,' the girl whispered and then everyone promptly forgot all about her because Cerise came into the room beaming all over her face, followed by a stunningly pretty girl with tanned skin, long blonde hair, a leather coat slung over her school uniform and dark glasses.

'Ah,' Mrs Mackie said, looking suitably stunned.

'It's Araminta Eversage!' Cerise announced, and then there was a pause when we could have done with a fanfare of trumpets.

'Araminta Eversage?' Mrs Mackie said in disbelief. She consulted her papers. 'I thought your name was Jane Hutt.'

The girl frowned a little. 'That's the name I was born with but I don't use it professionally. Professionally I'm known as Araminta Eversage. It sounds more special, don't you think?'

Mrs Mackie quickly recovered herself. 'I don't know about that,' she said, 'but I do know that *here* you'll be known as Jane Hutt.' I nudged Fleur gleefully; Mrs Mackie would sort *her* out all right.

'Now, you put your coat in one of these

lockers,' Cerise said, taking the coat off Jane/ Araminta's shoulders, 'and I've chosen this desk for you over here next to mine.'

'Thank you, Cerise, that's quite enough,' Mrs Mackie said, 'perhaps you'll go and sit down now.' Her eyes followed Cerise as she walked to her desk, 'and by the way, you're allowed to wear tights in this cold weather, but only navy-blue or cream ones, not cerise-coloured. And before you tell me, I know you always like to wear something cerise because of your name, but as I've told you until I'm blue in the face, cerise isn't one of our school colours.'

The new girl hung her leather coat up in her locker and as she crossed the classroom, Mrs Mackie whipped her dark glasses of her nose. 'I don't think you'll be needing dark glasses in school, Jane,' she said. 'You're not a registered blind person, are you?'

Jane pushed out her bottom lip. 'The sunlight hurts my eyes,' she said.

'Well, luckily it's not too sunny inside,' Mrs Mackie said, 'so perhaps you'd like to collect your glasses on the way home. And please note that you're supposed to be sitting in the classroom and waiting for me at eight-forty, not nine o'clock. I know all about making dramatic entrances but I hope we're not going to have one from you every morning.'

Looking rebellious, Jane thrust her hands into her pockets and slouched towards where Cerise was sitting. Now she had her coat off,

18

I could see that her school skirt was as short and tight as Cerise's.

'We'll speak about your skirt later, but right now I'll also have your earrings,' Mrs Mackie said. 'No doubt you've seen a copy of the school prospectus which clearly states that we only allow small plain stud ones.'

'Perhaps you'd like me to take everything off and start again?' Jane said sarcastically, and we all squirmed in our seats with delight.

'That won't be necessary,' Mrs Mackie said smoothly, 'although you will have to tie your hair back.'

'I can't believe this!' Jane said, and she stamped her way over to Cerise and slouched in her seat sulkily.

Fleur scribbled something in the back of her rough book and passed it over to me. It said: *I think we're going to have some fun this term . . .*

Chapter Two

THE STAR, THE MOUSE
AND THE RABBITS

'Hello, Fatso,' Alison said, coming up behind us in the lunch queue and slapping Fleur on the back. 'Been stuffing your fat face over Christmas?'

'No, I haven't, actually,' Fleur said. 'In fact, I've lost weight.'

'She's miles thinner!' I said to Alison. 'Anyone with half an eye can see that.'

'Watch it!' Alison said nastily, narrowing her eyes. 'You just be careful how you talk to me.'

Fleur and I nudged each other and both shut up, not wanting to get on the wrong side of Alison this early in the term.

'Where's the mouse person?' Fleur asked me.

'Marie?' I shrugged. 'Don't know. She was

sitting behind us in history and then she just seemed to disappear.'

'Went into a little hole in the skirting board, perhaps,' Fleur said. She didn't mean it unkindly. Fleur just liked a vivid phrase.

We sat down at one of the dining room tables, both with a new-this-term pizza. The kitchens had been modernised in the holidays and they now had what they called a 'Fast Food Bar', where they sold hamburgers and hot dogs as well as pizzas.

Alison joined us – she couldn't find any-one else to be nasty to, I suppose – and then Philippa came up with a gloating smile on her face. 'I've got a postcard from Annabel!' she said.

'Where d'you get that from?' I asked.

'Mrs Mackie's just passed it on. It arrived at the school secretary's office with a letter explaining that she wouldn't be here until later this term.'

'Where is she, then?'

'Bermuda.' She looked at the postcard again. 'No, Barbados.'

'What's she doing there?'

'She's on holiday, of course.'

Fleur and I both tried to read the card for ourselves but Philippa held it away from us and read it so we couldn't see it. 'Her mother and father have taken a house there for six weeks!'

'Some people have all the luck,' Fleur said.

'She says it's absolutely heavenly and she's

getting a wonderful tan.' She stowed the postcard safely in her pocket. 'Isn't she lucky. Imagine going out there.' She gazed thoughtfully into space, 'I wonder if she's ever allowed to take a friend when she goes on holiday . . .'

'Well, I bet she wouldn't be allowed to take any of us,' Fleur said. She grinned at me. 'Not since Mickey tried to drown Annabel's mother in her own swimming pool.'

I saw a movement outside and pointed towards the swing doors. 'Here come Jane and Cerise!'

Everyone on our table, Alison, Philippa and the twins turned to look, and those on the two adjoining tables looked to see what we were looking at, so in the end there were about thirty girls all turning and staring at Jane and whispering excitedly to each other.

When she saw everyone looking she preened herself, flicked her blonde hair backwards off her face and assumed a wide smile. She'd had to tie her hair back during the morning – Mrs Mackie had supplied an elastic band – but it was down again all over her shoulders now. She walked to the food counter very slowly, as if she was a model on a catwalk at a fashion show.

'She's preparing to meet her public,' Fleur said. 'Are we ready for her?'

'Have we got a red carpet?' I asked.

Jasbir looked indignant. 'I think you're being very horrible,' she said. 'She's lovely and I think we're lucky to have her here. *I'm* going to go on television when I'm older.'

'Don't be stupid!' Arina said immediately. 'You wouldn't be any good on television, you can't even read read things out in class!'

'I can!' Jasbir said.

'You go all red! You hate people looking at you!'

'It would be different on television,' Jasbir said. 'I'm going to be a newsreader.'

'How could you!' Arina said, 'You could never pronounce all those long words! You wouldn't have me there to ask all the time, you know.'

'Who needs you!' Jasbir said hotly, 'I jolly well bet I'd get on a lot better without . . .'

'Sssh!' I said. 'Cerise is looking all round for a suitable table for Jane. Try and look as if you're ready to have a famous person sitting with you.'

'I'm surprised she's having lunch in here with us ordinary people,' Fleur said in a low voice. 'I thought the TV studios would at least send in a mobile food unit.'

'Make a space on this table!' Philippa said. 'Jane can come and sit with us.' She was pink-faced with excitement – all morning she and Cerise had been practically fighting with each other to 'look after' Jane.

'She may not want to sit with us,' I said. We'd tried to talk to Jane at break but she'd been so moody, muttering about how awful the school was and how she wasn't going to stay a minute longer than she had to. When we'd asked her about her TV parts she'd said she was under contract not to reveal anything. 'I'd have all the newspapers after me if I started gossiping!' she'd said.

We didn't really understand why she was at our school at all, although the rumour was that her mum and dad had moved nearby and, because she was getting too big-headed, they wanted her to go to an ordinary school instead of the stage school she was at.

'Clear a space, please!' Cerise said, coming away from the food counter. 'Araminta wants to sit here.'

'Ooh, yippee! It's our lucky day!' Fleur said under her breath, but we all moved up a bit to let her in.

Even though I didn't think I was going to particularly like her, it was exciting having her there and I couldn't wait to get home and tell mum. She hadn't been in that many episodes of *Village Life* as far as I could remember, but I'd seen her in an advertisement – toothpaste or something – so she was a *bit* famous.

Cerise sat herself down on the very end of the table and Jane settled herself down in the middle like a queen sitting on a throne in front of her subjects.

'Jane, is it really different here to being at stage school?' Philippa asked. 'It must have been really awful for you to leave all your friends. Were there lots of other girls there who've been on TV? Would we know any of them?'

We all leaned forward to listen to the reply, but Jane didn't say anything, just took a neat bite out of her cheese sandwich and stared straight ahead of her.

'Is she deaf?' I whispered to Fleur.

'Maybe,' she said. 'Perhaps it's all the noise in the studios.'

Cerise coughed politely. 'Araminta has decided not to answer to the name of Jane,' she announced, pleased to know something that Philippa, who looked like being her main rival in the Araminta Eversage fan club, didn't know.

Philippa then repeated her first question, this time calling her Araminta, and Jane smiled and put down her sandwich.

'Since you've asked, yes, it's absolutely ghastly to have been made to come to this place,' she said, tossing her long hair all over the place. 'However, I don't intend to stay long.'

I wanted to ask her why she'd had to come here anyway, but I didn't see why I had to call her Araminta. I thought it was a really silly name and, besides, it was already sounding too much like 'Gardeners' Question Time' on our table without *me* joining in.

'Araminta, are you in any episodes of *Village Life* soon?' Philippa said, 'only I'd like to make sure I record them.'

Jane pursed her lips. 'No, that's the ridiculous thing,' she said with another toss of her hair, 'I'm not allowed to attend the studios to do any recordings in term time; my episodes have to be done during the holidays. Occasionally I do a little weekend work, of course.'

'Ooh, how exciting!' Philippa said, looking spellbound at actually being in her presence.

'Do tell us a little bit about Patrick Parker,' Cerise said with a sigh. 'Is he as gorgeous as he looks?'

'Oh, he's an absolute darling!' Jane said airily.

'Will you . . . d'you think you might be able to get me a signed photograph?' asked Cerise.

'Oh, of course,' Jane said. 'Any time!'

'So what are you working on now, then, Araminta?' said Philippa. 'Or do you just concentrate on school work during the term?'

'Oh no!' Jane said disdainfully, 'school work is the last thing I'm bothered about. No, my agent sends me scripts to read and I have auditions to attend.' She looked round to make sure we were all hanging on her every word, 'I'm going for a crucial audition next week – a very important cat food advertisement.'

Fleur and I kicked each other under the table and Fleur twitched some imaginary whiskers and made me giggle. I was just going to say something to her in meow-talk when Mrs Mackie strode up to us leading Marie/Mouse by the hand.

'Girls! I'm surprised at you, I really am!' she said.

We all looked round at her except Jane, who carried on nibbling daintily at her sandwich.

'We have two *new* girls, you know, and as exciting as it is to have a TV star in our presence . . .' she said this in her specially sarcastic voice '. . . you mustn't neglect our other new girl.'

Marie stood to one side of her, hanging her head and looking more mouse-like than ever. It was weird, until Fleur had mentioned her at lunchtime I'd honestly forgotten we had anyone else new in the class. She hadn't said a word all morning and I didn't even remember seeing her around at break.

'Manners, please, girls! Will someone kindly look after Marie. How can the poor girl get lunch if no one tells her where the dining-room is?'

'I'll take her up to the counter, Mrs Mackie!' Alison said, and though Mrs Mackie looked doubtful at this unlikely combination, she let Alison lead her off. Alison was always creepy when there were any teachers around. If you didn't know what she was really like when there *weren't* teachers about you might have taken her for a goody-goody like Alice.

'Ah, I see you've lost your elastic band, Jane!' Mrs Mackie said, suddenly seeming to notice the blonde hair spilling all over Jane's shoulders, She pulled another one out of her pocket. 'Pull your hair back,please. I'm sure the girls don't want blonde hairs all over their meals.'

'I don't mind!' Cerise said in her silliest voice, and Mrs Mackie shook her head, rolled her eyes and walked away. As soon as she'd gone, Jane took off the elastic band again and shook her hair out.

'You shouldn't be made to wear one of those elastic bands,' Cerise said, 'they tear the hair dreadfully. Mummy never lets me wear anything which might damage mine.'

'But you've had a perm!' Arina said. 'Doesn't that damage it?'

'It's only a very soft one,' Cerise said. 'It gives my hair body. It's baby fine, you see.' She put out a hand and touched Jane's long thick hair. 'I wish I had lovely strong hair like you, though,' she said wistfully, then added, 'does Patrick like girls with straight blonde hair, d'you know?'

The twins went off, bickering about the ownership of a ruler, and Alison and Mouse came back from the food counter and sat down.

'Sorry!' I said to Mouse. 'I think we just forgot all about you.'

'That's all right,' she said. She had a tiny little voice and spoke with a country accent so it was difficult to make out what she was saying.

'It won't happen again,' Alison said in an important voice. 'I'm going to look after Marie from now on.'

Fleur gave me a meaningful look and I gave her one back. Who'd ever want *Alison* looking after them?

'Of course, if I get this part in the cat commercial it could change my life!' Jane said loudly from the other end of the table and we all looked back towards her. 'It's a long-running one, you see, like the Oxo ones. I could end up being completely famous. My face will be known nationally, from coast to coast.'

'Ooh,' breathed Cerise and Philippa together.

Fleur and I got up and went to get our coats to go outside.

'I think Philippa's found someone else to shadow, don't you?' Fleur asked.

I nodded. 'Annabel's not here so I suppose she's got to have someone.'

'Should be fun when Annabel comes back, then,' Fleur said.

After lunch we had Computing, with Miss Philby. There weren't enough computers in the class to have one each, so we shared between two or three. I started off sharing with Fleur, but wasn't allowed to stay with her for long.

'Now, what do we remember from last term?' Miss Philby asked when our computers were switched on and we were all ready to go.

'Not a lot!' I called out. I quite liked playing games on computers, and messing about making things appear and disappear, but I wasn't very keen on anything else.

Miss Philby looked over at me. 'Yes, well, in your case, Mickey, I'm not surprised. In fact, I'd be surprised if you learnt *anything* last term. 'If I remember you spent most of your time here typing messages to Fleur.'

Fleur and I grinned. We really liked Miss Philby because she was young and pretty and we knew she sang in a group at weekends.

'I think I'll move you,' Miss Philby said to me. 'You can go with Erica and – what's your name, love?' she asked Mouse, who replied 'Marie' in a tiny voice. 'Su, you can share with Fleur,' Miss Philby added.

Miss Philby sat herself down at the front of the class on a master console, told us to switch on our screens, then gave us instructions on how to find the worksheet she'd prepared.

'Now, its taken me ages and ages to prepare the worksheet for you, so please don't put any commands into the computer until I tell you. All these computers are linked and I'd hate to lose a whole day's work.'

'Now, the first thing you've got to master is how to add extra information to your worksheet, and then we'll learn how to delete it. Would everyone first of all press the button on the far right . . .' And she droned on, slowly and tediously, while I yawned and tried to catch Fleur's attention. I'd been using my brothers' computer for ages now and could play all sorts of games on it, and this was just so boring . . .

'Can you remember all this from last year?' Erica asked in a whisper.

'Course!' I said. 'It's dead easy.'

'We didn't have computers at my last school,'

Mouse said, 'so I don't really understand what she's talking about.'

'Oh, they're just like typewriters only they do a few extra things,' I said airily, 'you mustn't be scared of them.' She didn't look convinced, so I added, 'I can draw a line of rabbits on my brothers' computer and print them out.'

'Go on then,' Erica said.

Miss Philby was still droning on, so I jabbed my finger on the capital O. 'First you do a row of Os,' I said, 'and then a row of Ms on top of that – for their ears, and then . . .'

'Are you paying attention, Mickey?' Miss Philby asked suddenly, and I looked up and nodded emphatically. 'Because I'll be coming round in a moment to see what you've got up on your screen.'

'Crumbs,' I said under my breath, and I jabbed at the Delete button to make the half-rabbits disappear. They didn't want to go, though. I jabbed again, then at the escape button, then the backspace, then delete again, then all three at once, and suddenly our screen went blank – phat! – just like that. Not only that but all the other screens also went phat.

Miss Philby let out a sudden scream. Her screen had gone phat, too.

'How did that happen? Who did that? Who was pressing something they shouldn't have done?' she said, standing up and waving her arms around a lot. 'I'll absolutely kill them if I find out!'

Mouse looked at me nervously out of the corner of her eye.

'I'd better show you how to do a row of rabbits some other time . . .' I said very quietly indeed. And there I'd been on the bus telling myself I was going to be lots better this term. Well, I hadn't got off to a very good start . . .

Chapter Three
THE BATTLE OF
ARINA AND JASBIR

It was break and Fleur and I were making
our way outside to the playground, but going
slowly because it was very cold and frosty
out.

Cerise and Jane were in a huddle by the
radiator, bent over a big bag of make-up
Jane had brought in with her, and every
now and again looking out of the window
with quick, darting glances. It was obvious
now why Cerise had picked them a desk
next to the window – they had the best view
of the boys' school playground from there.
Whenever we had an indoor break or whenever we had an actual lesson in our own
classroom, they were to be found staring
out of the window hoping to see someone
exciting.

Boys were the only interest that Philippa didn't share with Cerise and Jane. She pretended they were, though, so as not to get left out.

'Ooh, what a gorgeous colour lipstick!' Cerise was saying to Jane. 'I can never find a lovely pink like that anywhere.'

'It's special TV lipstick,' Jane said – she always said whatever she had was 'selected specially for TV' or 'unobtainable by the general public'. 'It's extra long-lasting. It has to be in case we have to kiss anyone.'

'Ooh,' Cerise breathed longingly, and opened her beauty box and gazed at the picture of Patrick Parker she now kept stuck inside. 'I know who I'd like to kiss if I was on the telly.' She looked at Jane. 'I suppose . . . well, d'you think I might have a chance? I mean, do they ever want girls like me as extras for background parts?'

Jane looked at her pityingly. 'Afraid not. They always take extras from drama schools. You've got to be trained, you see. You can't just have any old person appearing on telly just because they feel like it.'

'I suppose not,' said Cerise, crestfallen.

'And let's face it, most people have got about as much star quality as a frozen chicken,' Jane added, and Cerise nodded sadly.

'Are you two coming outside?' I asked. 'You're bound to get caught if you don't.' However long we stretched the time it took to put on our duffle coats, we had to disappear in the end because Mrs Mackie usually came prowling about.

'We're staying in,' Jane said. 'I don't want to get my hands chapped in case I'm called back for a second audition for the cat food advertisement.'

'Why don't you wear gloves when you're out?' Fleur asked. 'They'd be all right then.'

'Oh, that's not enough protection,' Jane said.

'Why isn't it?' asked Fleur.

Jane looked at her witheringly. 'You wouldn't understand,' she said, 'no one would unless they were actually on television themselves. My hands have to be perfect.' She hoisted herself on to the radiator and stared out of the window and Cerise shut the lid of her beauty box and joined her.

'Oh, Araminta, there's that boy from third year!' Cerise cooed, pointing into the distance where a vague figure could be seen standing by a tree. 'I'm sure he's looking over here.'

'Where?' Jane squinted desperately to try and see. She needed to wear glasses – she couldn't read things when the teachers wrote on the board – but she wouldn't, of course. She said it would ruin her image.

'There. Next to the tree.'

'D'you think he knows it's me?' Jane asked. 'D'you think he's recognised me?'

'Oh, I'm sure he has. I expect they all know you're here and they want to catch a glimpse of you,' Cerise gushed.

Fleur and I dragged ourselves away from

this two-girl appreciation society and straggled into the corridor just as Mrs Mackie strode up with her glasses slipping off her nose.

'Not outside yet? Get going, will you! Break will be over if you don't get a move on.'

That was what we'd intended, of course. We carried on walking but, when we reached the corner, stopped so we could hear what she said to the other two.

'For goodness' sake! Why are you two still inside?' she barked at them.

'It's too cold out, Mrs Mackie,' said Cerise. She gave a pathetic sniff, 'and I think I'm getting a nasty head cold.'

'Then a breath of air will do you good. And get off those radiators at once, you'll get piles.'

'Piles of what?' we heard Cerise ask innocently, and Fleur and I stuffed our hands over our mouths to try and keep in the giggles.

'I don't know what the continual attraction of this window is for you two girls,' Mrs Mackie went on, and then she must have looked out of the window herself because she said, 'Oh, I see. The boys' school.' She tutted, 'I've come to expect that sort of silly behaviour from the third years, but usually my first years are much more sensible about boys. You can take my word for it, though, that the boys aren't interested in *you*. Boys have hobbies, they don't just live to come to school and stare at you two.'

'Please Mrs Mackie, we can't go outside because of Araminta's hands,' Cerise said.

'Do you mean *Jane's* hands?' Mrs Mackie asked. 'Well, *Jane's* hands, as we can all see, are on *Jane's* arms. I don't understand how anything concerning Jane's hands can possibly affect you, Cerise.'

'But Mrs Mackie, it's her cat food advertisement . . .' we heard Cerise begin, and then we had to miss the rest because Mrs Evans, our science teacher, came out of her room and chivvied us along.

A bit later Cerise and Jane appeared in the playground. Cerise was sniffing falsely and Jane had her school jumper sleeves pulled right down over her hands and looked rebellious.

'Cerise is sillier than ever this term,' Arina said, coming up with her twin. 'That Jane has really set her off.'

'I wish you wouldn't call her Jane,' Jasbir said. 'Araminta doesn't like it.'

'Tough!' Arina said.

'And anyway it's not Araminta who's set her off at all,' Jasbir said. 'Cerise was stupid to begin with.'

'She's twice as stupid now that she's got that precious television star for a friend. I've not seen her on the box lately, anyway. I think the television companies have dumped her!'

'You only haven't seen her because you wouldn't look!' Jasbir said, turning on Arina indignantly. 'She was on the other night and you deliberately went out of the room!'

'It isn't as if she can even act!'

'Oh, I suppose you know all about it, do you? Let me tell you that . . .' Jasbir started hotly, and Fleur and I exchanged a look and crept away. The twins' quarrels were known to go on for hours sometimes.

When the bell went we made our way back in – going extra slowly again because it was maths – and caught up with Mouse along the way. I felt sorry for her because we'd all made our best friends by the time she'd arrived, and she'd got lumbered with Alison, who wasn't any sort of substitute for a best friend. Mouse was as quiet and timid as ever, even though she knew us better now. The teachers had had to stop her reading out loud in class because, even when she was speaking as loudly as she possibly could, no one could hear her.

'Are you all right?' I asked, because she looked a bit more mouse-like than usual.

'Fine,' she said quietly, not sounding fine at all.

'Is Alison behaving herself?' Fleur asked. 'She's nor . . . er . . . borrowing any bars of chocolate or crisps from you or anything, is she?'

Mouse went red but didn't say anything.

'She took stuff from all of us last term,' I said. 'But as far as I know she hasn't tried it on with anyone this year.'

'Well, actually, she did . . . she's asked me

for biscuits and stuff,' Mouse said, 'and I didn't like to say no.'

'Well, if she does it again – tell us,' I said. 'We thought of a good trick to stop her last year.'

Fleur nodded. 'And we can always think of another one. She's a nasty bit of work, that Alison.'

As if to confirm what she was saying, Alison herself came down the corridor. 'Wotcha, fat girl!' she called to Fleur. 'How's your skinny friend?'

Fleur and I increased speed towards our own classroom to get out of Alison's range and get our maths books out of our lockers.

'We'll have to warn the others that Alison's up to her old tricks,' I said.

'I bet she's copying from Mouse in class, too.'

'D'you think so?' I asked.

Fleur nodded. 'You know what a dimbo Alison is – well, she hasn't been hauled out in class for any bad work lately, has she?'

I shook my head. 'I never thought of that.'

The twins appeared at the lockers to collect their maths books and put back their breaktime drinks beakers. Their mum made them a special yogurt and milk drink to have at break and they always brought them in blue plastic beakers with sealed lids.

Just as they were putting them away, Jasbir pounced on Arina's beaker. 'That's mine!' she said. 'Mine is the older one!'

'No, it's not!' Arina said, 'Don't start all that again.'

She'd once explained to me that in their last school they'd taken the same drinks in every day and Jasbir had a pink beaker, Arina a blue. Suddenly, though, Jasbir had gone off the pink beaker and wanted one like Arina's. Their mother had then bought an identical blue one, but Jasbir still wasn't satisfied, she wanted the old beaker, which was a slightly faded blue, and Arina said that every so often there was a battle at home over who was having which blue beaker.

'I will have that one if I want it!' Jasbir said.

'No, you won't. You jolly well listen to me, Jasbir, I'm going to be really cross if you keep on about this.'

'And I'm going to be really cross if I don't get that beaker!' Jasbir suddenly squealed. 'Give it to me at once!'

'I won't!'

'Give it to me or . . . or I'll pull your hair!' Jasbir said, and so saying, she put out her hand and grabbed Arina's topknot.

She pulled as hard as she could, several hairpins fell to the floor and Arina screamed at the top of her voice – just as Mrs Mackie came in ready to take her second year history class.

'Arina! Jasbir!' she shouted. 'What is going on?'

The twins, shocked into silence, turned to face a furious Mrs Mackie.

'This is intolerable,' she said. 'Your continual squabbling has been getting me down and upsetting everyone else, and now we have actual fighting – fighting in my class! Such a dreadful thing has never ever happened before.'

Arina and Jasbir just stood there, looking frightened and breathing fast. Jasbir still had some wisps of pulled-off hair in her hand.

'Sorry,' Arina said.

'Yes. Sorry,' Jasbir put in quickly.

'I'm afraid sorry will not do any longer,' Mrs Mackie said crisply. 'The whole class is being disrupted by your constant bickering.' She paused then went on, 'I really think the two of you will work – and play – better if you are split up and put in different classes.'

We all gasped at this but Mrs Mackie just went on, 'I told the headmistress when you first joined the school that twins worked better when they were separated, but she insisted that you were put together. Now, I'm sorry to say that I've been proved right. Arina, I'm going to make arrangements for you to go into Mrs Clark's – the other first year class.'

Jasbir burst into tears, Arina looked shocked. 'When, Mrs Mackie?' she asked.

'Right now,' she said. 'Come along.' And with that she swept out of the classroom. Arina looked at the rest of us, made a helpless gesture, then followed.

'Good riddance,' Alison said. 'I'm fed up

with hearing them rowing all the time. It gets on my nerves.'

'But ... it won't be the same with just one twin in the class,' I said, looking at a sobbing Jasbir.

'That Mrs Mackerel wants sorting out,' Jane said loudly, suddenly butting into the general amazement and confusion.

I looked at her in surprise; it wasn't like her to stand up for anyone else; she'd only ever spoken up before when it was something involving *her*.

'The teachers at my drama school treated you as adults, not as babies,' she said loftily. 'I don't know how you lot stand it – all the fuss about uniform and not wearing big earrings or different coloured socks or anything. And as for being forced outside in all weathers – that's ridiculous.'

'It might be ridiculous but it's school rules and always has been,' said Alice in her best head girl's voice.

Jane ignored her. 'I don't know why you lot don't stand up to old Mackerel-features and get your own back,' she continued. 'I'm going to ... just you wait and see.'

Chapter Four
HOUSEPOINTS

The next morning before register we didn't see Arina at all – she'd gone straight into Mrs Clark's class – but we were faced with a red-eyed and crying Jasbir. She said she hadn't slept a bit and if Arina had to be in Mrs Clark's class, she wanted to be there, too.

'Maybe you'll get used to it,' I said, trying to comfort her. 'It might be better. You'll still see Arina at break and at lunchtime and you're together out of school all the time anyway.'

'It's not the same,' she hiccuped. 'We've never been separated before. I don't like it . . . it doesn't feel right.'

Jasbir sat and cried all through register and at first Mrs Mackie ignored her, then she got exasperated and asked how long it was going to go on for and couldn't she control herself?

We were just waiting for the bell for first class to ring when the school secretary came in. She whispered something in a low voice to Mrs Mackie and they went outside.

Philippa darted from her seat behind Cerise and Jane and peered out of the small window in the door to see where she'd gone.

'There's a man talking to Mrs Mackie!' she reported.

Jasbir looked up. 'Is it my dad?' she said, and she wiped her face with a soggy tissue and got up to have a look.

'It is!' she said excitedly, as she sat back down again. 'I hope he's come to get Arina back.'

'He's talking very seriously to Mrs Mackie,' Philippa reported from the door. She was in her element as class spy. 'Mrs Mackie looks reluctant . . . she's shaking her head . . . Now he's saying something very sternly and waving his arms about a bit. Now she's sighing and nodding and . . .' she suddenly leapt back from the door, '. . . now she's coming back in!'

But Mrs Mackie didn't come back in. We sat there for a moment and then Philippa got up and had another look out of the door. 'There's no one out there,' she said, 'I bet she's gone straight to Mrs Clark's class.'

We all sat chatting and wondering what the twins' dad had said and a moment later Mrs Mackie came back into the class with Arina.

Arina sat back in her old seat next to Jasbir,

grinning all over her face, and Jasbir practically squeezed her to death. You would have thought they'd been separated for weeks, not just fifteen minutes.

Mrs Mackie looked round the class sternly. 'This is much against my better judgement,' she said, 'but Arina and Jasbir's father seems to think it will affect the twins and the rest of their family so adversely, that I've had to give in. I've told him, though, that I will not stand for anymore fisticuffs in class.' She waggled a warning finger at Jasbir and Arina. 'If it ever happens again, the separation will be permanent — and I won't be persuaded to change my mind. No, not even if your entire family comes up here with sob stories.'

'No, Mrs Mackie,' the twins said obediently, and I saw them happily punching each other underneath the desks.

We all went off to maths then, where there was another, even bigger, bit of excitement involving Jane, Cerise and Philippa. Up till then Cerise seemed to have won the competition to be Jane's best friend; she'd got a permanent seat next to her in our own classroom and managed to be right next to her everywhere else by sticking to her like glue and refusing to be shaken off. Sometimes Philippa got fed up with this, though, and tried to edge her out, but wherever they were there was usually some sort of aggro going on between the two of them.

We were just waiting for Mrs Taylor to come in and Fleur and I were just discussing whether, if she had her hair cut really short, it would make her look fatter or thinner, when a scuffle broke out in the doorway between Philippa and Cerise – both of them were trying to get through it at the same time as Jane was. The scuffle continued all the way across the class, with each of them jostling the other and saying that they were going to sit with Jane and the other one had better watch out.

'But I always sit next to Araminta in maths!' Cerise said.

'All the more reason for it to be my turn!' said Philippa.

'But Araminta wants me to sit next to her as usual,' Cerise said, and turned to Jane, 'Don't you?'

Jane shrugged. I think she like playing off one of them against the other. 'I don't care. Just decide between you and get on with it, will you?'

We were all out of our seats by this time, all the better to watch the fun.

'But when I asked you before register this morning you said I could sit next to you!' Philippa said. 'I asked specially.'

'Well, hard luck, because I'm sitting down right now!' said Cerise. She was fluffy and silly, but she could be determined when she wanted to be – and she was dead determined that no one was going to take her darling Araminta away from her.

'That's what you think!' Philippa said, and she pulled Cerise's jumper hard and tried to pull her off the seat.

'My jumper! You'll pull it all out of shape!' Cerise squealed. 'Take your hands off it.'

'I will if you get up!' Philippa said, and giving one last vicious tug, she tugged Cerise right onto the floor. Cerise set up a big howl and in the middle of it all Mrs Taylor, the maths teacher, arrived.

The rest of us went as quiet as mice but Cerise, still yelling, lay sprawled on the ground where she'd fallen, her cerise-coloured plastic headband all crooked.

Philippa stood there trying to look innocent as Mrs Taylor strode over to their side of the room and stared at the two girls with pursed lips.

Mrs Taylor was very strict. We reckoned that the harder the subject or the lesson was, the stricter the person who taught it seemed to be – and maths was hardest of all.

'I'm not interested in hearing the reasons for this disgraceful behaviour,' Mrs Taylor said, 'I expect it was something extremely stupid.' She looked hard at Jane as if she knew she was at the bottom of things. None of the teachers liked her much because she never stopped showing off in class. 'No, I'm not going to waste time,' she went on, 'Philippa Biggs and Cerise Mills, lose one housepoint each.'

Everyone gasped and Mrs Taylor clapped

her hands. 'That's enough. Back to your places everyone, and open your books at page 97.'

Fleur and I made gruesome faces at each other. Losing housepoints was terrible – you only lost them for the direst things – and none of us had lost any during the whole of last term. Mrs Mackie had let it be known that she would be severely displeased if any of 'her' first years did anything bad enough to merit losing any. Her old first years had behaved beautifully at all times under all circumstances, of course, and she expected us to do the same.

Cerise stopped wailing and, looking shocked about the housepoint but unable to resist giving Philippa a triumphant smirk, scrambled back on her seat next to Jane. Philippa, looking miserable, sat behind them and as close to Jane as she could get. We all opened our books at page 97.

We discussed losing housepoints at break. We could only remember one being lost last term and that had been by someone in the Fifth. If you *did* lose one you had your name read out by the head in assembly at the end of the month – in a couple of days' time – and she – Miss Harmer – would make you look as small and stupid as possible while everyone else, the whole school, turned to stare at you. It was a real nightmare . . .

Two days later we were all sitting in assembly with eyes front, faces scrubbed, socks pulled up and skirts pulled down over our knees. We'd sat through the notices and Miss Harmer's usual little reminders about wearing make up, ('I've seen some girls who look more as if they're going to a discotheque not to school,' she'd said).

'And now we come to the most serious part of our assembly,' Miss Harmer said, 'when I will read out to you the names of girls who have lost points this month.'

Her eyes scanned the seated rows of us and we all straightened ourselves a bit more and tried to look completely and utterly good. Miss Harmer was old, but not cosy-grandma old – nasty-witch-in-fairy-stories old. Very scary, she was.

'This month I have to report that I have two girls who have lost housepoints,' Miss Harmer went on in a doom-laden voice. 'They were waiting in their class for a teacher, but sadly they couldn't be trusted to wait quietly and, do you know what happened?' She stopped speaking and looked at us so hard that I felt shivery. 'They started fighting – yes, *fighting* in a classroom. Two girls from Park Wood actually *fighting*!'

She shook her head and her eyes went more witchy. 'Perhaps the most shameful part of this whole affair,' she said, 'is that the girls are both in the first year. Never before has such a terrible thing occured.'

Mrs Mackie sat next to us, quietly bristling and fuming to herself. She'd been horrified, and at her most icily cutting when she'd heard about the housepoints, saying she was thoroughly ashamed of Philippa and Cerise and that they'd disgraced her in the eyes of the school. It had all gone over Cerise's head a bit; whenever Mrs Mackie said anything she just sat there smiling her silly little smile and fingering the pink bow in her hair or her pink plastic beads or whatever, but Philippa was just the opposite; she hated being on the wrong side of Mrs Mackie and would keep putting her hand up in class to give books out or offer to do some other creepy thing to get back on the right side of her.

What made things really bad as far as Mrs Mackie was concerned was that she and Miss Harmer hated each other, and everyone knew it. One of the older girls had told me that, years ago, they'd both wanted to be head and both had had campaigns to make the other look unsuitable. Miss Harmer had won, of course, and had been head for millions of years now, but neither of them had ever forgiven the other one for the things they'd said at the time, and neither ever lost an opportunity to pay off old scores.

Miss Harmer sighed deeply and dramatically. 'Now,' she said, 'would Cerise Mills and Philippa Biggs stand up and let the school see what sort of girls can actually fight in class.'

The whole school looked towards us first years, ready to relish every moment of the drama. There was a movement in the line behind me and Cerise and Philippa, who were sitting one each side of Jane, slowly stood up. Both had their shoulders hunched and looked at the ground, and Cerise had her eyes tightly closed as if she was trying to pretend she wasn't there at all. Her face was very pink.

'I hope you two girls are thoroughly ashamed of yourselves,' she started, while the rest of the school stared at them, nudged each other and whispered. 'By fighting like common hooligans you are bringing the name of Park Wood into disrepute and I believe that . . .' She stopped suddenly and her head jerked forward on her neck like a chicken's. 'What is that thing that girl is wearing in her hair?'

Cerise realised she was talking about her and opened her eyes.

'Yes, you, Cerise Mills, you. What is that pink object?'

'P . . . please, Miss Harmer, it's a hairslide,' Cerise said.

'And why are you wearing a coloured hairslide when you surely know what the school rules are?'

'Well, you see, because my name's Cerise I always like to . . .' Cerise began, and Alice, who was sitting next to her on the other side, jabbed at her foot urgently and Cerise took the hint and shut up.

'Take it off!' Erica hissed from behind her, and Cerise quickly lifted her hand and slipped off the offending slide.

'And does Mrs Mackie allow you to wear hair decorations?' Miss Harmer asked smoothly.

'Only when she doesn't see them,' Cerise said, and everyone roared with laughter. Cerise looked round the hall, pleased.

'No, I do not, Miss Harmer, as you well know,' said Mrs Mackie, and she, too, narrowed her eyes at Cerise. 'The hairslide must have escaped my notice this morning.'

'I see,' Miss Harmer said. 'Perhaps you will ensure that it doesn't escape it again. As you know, I have very strong views on jewellery and decoration on my girls.'

'Yes, Miss Harmer,' Mrs Mackie said in a rather bored voice.

'Well, as I was saying, I sincerely hope this sort of thing, this terrible fighting in class, will never occur again while I am headmistress here. If you two girls are ever involved in . . .'

Her head jerked forward again and we all froze, wondering what she'd seen now.

'What *is* that girl wearing – that girl sitting between Cerise Mills and Philippa Biggs. It surely can't be sunglasses.'

All eyes then moved on to Jane – who sat there looking straight ahead of her – and *actually wearing sunglasses*! Those who couldn't see craned their necks, some girls kneeled up to see better, and an excited buzz broke out round the hall.

'She wasn't wearing them when we came in – she must have just slipped them on,' I whispered to Fleur.

'Look at Mrs Mackie!' she whispered back.

I looked. Mrs Mackie was white-faced with

anger. She got up, strode between the lines of girls and snatched the sunglasses off Jane's nose.

'I confiscated those and told you never to wear them again!' she said, and she was in such a rage her voice was shaking. 'How dare you wear them to assembly!'

'Excuse me, Mrs Mackie!' Jane's voice rose above everyone else's – I suppose it was her drama training. 'Those are not sunglasses, they are prescription glasses from the optician. I'm shortsighted and my eyes are sensitive to sun and strong studio lights. I have to wear them.'

Fleur and I were beside ourselves with excitement by now and looking, with delicious horror, from Mrs Mackie to Jane to Miss Harmer and back again.

'Well, in that case,' Miss Harmer said, 'of course you must have them back. I'm surprised you didn't realise they were prescription glasses, Mrs Mackie.'

Mrs Mackie looked as if she was going to burst a blood vessel. If she could have killed both Miss Harmer and Jane stone dead with a look, she would have done. She walked back to Jane and jabbed the glasses back on to her face.

Miss Harmer clapped her hands for silence. 'And now, girls, if you'll all face the front again,' she said, 'perhaps we can carry on. The two girls in disgrace can sit down – and they will both come and see me during the lunch hour to tell me exactly what the fight was about.'

Well, I don't think anyone heard any of the other notices read out in assembly, we were all too excited. Once it was over and, as Fleur remarked, Miss Harmer had gone off to catch the ten o'clock broomstick, we formed a giggling group outside.

'Mrs Mackie's face!' Jasbir said. 'I thought she was going to explode!'

'Wasn't Araminta wonderful?' Philippa said. 'She took all the attention on to herself so that Cerise and I hardly got told off for losing housepoints at all.'

'She wasn't doing it to help them,' I muttered to Fleur, 'she was just doing what she does best – showing off on a big scale.'

'The whole assembly just turned into a personal fight between Miss Harmer and Mrs Mackie!' Alice said, her eyes wide. 'My sister told me that they were always getting at each other when *she* was here. Wait until I tell her!'

'Actually,' Jane said loftily, 'I was just doing what I said I'd do – getting revenge on old Mackerel-face. Maybe she'll realise now that she can't treat me any way she likes and get away with it.'

We talked about the assembly all through morning lessons – well, as much as we could without getting caught – and all through break, too. The whole *school* was talking about Miss Harmer and Mrs Mackie's vendetta, and Jane and the sunglasses, as if by chance there had been anyone – perhaps in the sixth, or one of the gardeners – who didn't know we had a TV star amongst us, they jolly well knew then. As I said to Fleur, it was getting less and less like school and more and more like a TV soap all the time . . .

Chapter Five

I FIND SOMETHING I'M GOOD AT
– AND LOSE IT AGAIN

We were in the art room waiting for Miss Lemming. We all liked art because Miss Lemming was one of the young, nice teachers who'd told us that no one had to be 'good' at art – she said it in inverted commas just like that – to enjoy it. She said that art was all about having ideas. Another good point about her was that she never minded us chatting. Group discussions about on-going work were valuable, she always said, and she didn't seem to notice that we were never actually talking about on-going work. Everything but.

'Now, the first thing we're going to do is get the pottery animals you started last week ready for firing in the kiln,' she said. 'All the first year work is on that shelf over there,' she pointed, 'and if you've wrapped it up correctly then it should still be nice and damp to work on.'

'Perhaps mine's improved itself overnight,' Fleur said despondently. 'Last week everyone thought I'd made an elephant.'

'*I* thought you'd made an elephant,' I said. 'What was it then?'

'A hamster,' she said. 'I couldn't get the nose right.'

I giggled as I searched along the rows for mine. I knew I'd wrapped it up tightly enough, but the trouble was, all the wrapped bundles looked identical. I'd done a cat – nearly everyone had. Dogs were difficult because you had to get a particular type of dog, but a cat could be any old cat. You didn't have to have it balanced on legs, either, you could have it curled in a ball – no one could go wrong doing a pottery cat curled in a ball.

'Here's mine,' Fleur said, unwrapping her plastic and poking at a brown lumpy thing with a pottery tool.

'It *does* look more like an elephant,' I said, trying to work out which bit was which.

Fleur nodded. 'I think I might turn it into one.'

'You can't,' I said knowledgeably. 'You'd never get the trunk to stay on if you added it now. Miss Lemming said tail and things have got to be integral – if you add them on they just come off when you fire them.'

I moved along the shelves, searching. 'I can't find mine,' I muttered. 'It wasn't bad, either. I bet someone has taken a fancy to it.'

I eventually found a small wrapped parcel which had been left on the wrong shelf. It was my cat, all right – and it was looking even better than I remembered.

'I must have quite a talent for this,' I said, showing it off to Fleur. 'Look at this. Almost life-like, don't you think?'

'How can it be life-like if it's that small?' Fleur said.

'Well, you know what I mean.' I stroked it admiringly with a pottery tool. It had very delicate fur-marks all over which I could hardly remember doing, and a lovely fat bushy tail. 'This is what I mean by an *integral* tail,' I said importantly. 'This is part of the entire cat, see. It hasn't been stuck on as an afterthought.'

'Clever old you,' Fleur said, chopping viciously at her hamster.

I looked at my cat gloatingly. Perhaps I'd discovered the hidden talent I'd been looking for – I hadn't shone at anything so far – *pottery* was what I was going to be good at . . .

'I think I'll just make a few improvements,' I said, and I set to with the little pointed stick and scraped and poked away until my cat had big fat whiskers, four paws sticking out, and was sitting in a nice basket.

'That's not integral,' Fleur said when I'd finished. 'That basket is going to fall off.'

'I'm going to fire it separately,' I said.

'Don't you think those whiskers look funny?

And why are those feet sticking out like four blocks of wood? I think it was better before the improvements.'

'You don't know very much about art, do you?' I said. 'It's all about ideas.'

'Well, I think you've had too many,' Fleur said.

Miss Lemming had been marking some papers, now she came hunting along the shelves. 'I made something last week I wanted to show you,' she said. 'And now I can't find it. Has anyone seen a rather beautiful little fox cub? I'd marked his fur rather nicely and he was curled round with a nice bushy tail . . .'

I looked at Fleur, startled, and she looked back at me, but we all said no, we hadn't. Miss Lemming eventually found a round, faceless blob of brown clay.

'Whose is this?' she asked. 'I'm not sure what it's meant to be – a cat or a beach ball, probably.' She looked at me hard, 'Not yours, is it, Mickey? I seem to remember you making something about this size.'

I shook my head. 'Never seen it before in my life,' I said, cutting down on my cat's bushy tail a bit.

When we'd got our animals safely in the kiln and ready for firing, we started some big bright posters advertising the skiing trip – and Jane caused a fuss by refusing to use the strong-coloured paints because it would stain her hands.

'I'm going for my second audition for the

cat food advert tomorrow,' she said proudly to Miss Lemming, 'so my hands must look beautiful.' As she spoke she took some white cream out of her bag and began rubbing it in. 'I just hope they're not already ruined by that clay.' She looked round at the rest of us, 'I've got a photocall at nine o'clock in the morning, and before that a full manicure, so it's most important that my hands aren't stained. This advert could lead to a very important foreign contract, you see.'

But Miss Lemming wasn't the sort to be impressed by foreign contracts. 'If it's just a cat food advertisement they'll be concentrating on the tin more than your hands,' she said, 'so just you pick up that brush and get on with some work.'

Sulkily, Jane got on, although she refused point blank to use the black paint.

We were all having quite a nice messy time, actually, and Miss Lemming was talking to us about what it was like at art school. She was marking last week's work. We'd been sent outside with drawing boards to find bushes and trees and what she called *flora* to draw.

She suddenly stopped sorting through and gave an excited cry. 'Girls!' she said. 'Who ever did these? They're much smaller than the rest so they almost got lost behind the bigger sheets.'

We looked as she held up some small squares of grey paper covered all over with delicate, lacey white flowers. They certainly weren't mine – mine were the big clumsy trees that looked like lollipops and the grasses which looked like stick insects.

'These are absolutely beautiful,' Miss Lemming said, examining them closely. 'Cow parsley. Very delicate and lacey; lovely!'

She looked round the class. 'Is the talented owner going to own up?'

We all looked round at each other but no one said anything, and then someone put their hand up: *Mouse*! We all looked at her, amazed, and she went bright red.

'Well, Marie, you've certainly been keeping quiet about your skills,' Miss Lemming said, beaming at her. 'I didn't realise we had such an accomplished artist in the class.' She stared pinning the pictures onto the big board by the window. 'Have you had any special training?'

'No, but my father paints,' Mouse said in a low voice. 'I've always messed around copying him – ever since I was little.'

'I want you all to come up and look at Marie's work,' Miss Lemming said. 'See how perceptive she is . . . see how balanced these delicate little flowers are. It really shows remarkable talent in someone who's completely untrained.'

'Bet her father did them for her!' Jane hissed. She was niggled because Miss Lemming hadn't made a fuss of her and her audition.

'Don't be daft,' Fleur said. 'How could he? We were only outside for half an hour. D'you think he came along, did a few quick sketches and then passed them over the fence?'

Jane went quiet – only for a minute, though – then she asked Miss Lemming if she could possibly go to nurse as she had the beginnings of a headache. 'Such a bore,' she said, 'I often get one when I'm tense – like when I've got a big audition coming up, for instance.'

Miss Lemming wasn't any more interested in hearing about Jane's head than her hands, and seemed quite pleased at the prospect of getting rid of her. Both Cerise and Philippa wanted to take her to nurse, but when they both stood up straining their hands in the air and saying, *'Me! Can I take her please, Miss Lemming! Oh, let me!'* Miss Lemming immediately chose Erica to take her, which didn't please Jane a bit because Erica wasn't a fan.

We made quite a bit of fuss of Mouse at lunchtime and she brought out her sketch pad and did some clever little cartoon sketches of a few of us which we stuck on the front of our rough books. She was really good.

I caught her on her way in. 'How's Alison being?' I asked.

'Just the same,' she answered.

'Still pinching stuff? Shall I tell the others – see if we can think of something to stop her?'

'If you can,' she said doubtfully. 'Won't she really get nasty if she knows I've talked to you, though?'

'Not if we all stick together,' I said. 'I'll see if Fleur can think of anything . . .'

After lunch we all trooped back into our classroom to find a surprise waiting for us: *Annabel*!

'Hi!' she said, sitting on Mrs Mackie's desk and swinging her legs. 'I thought I'd surprise everyone.'

She looked really good. She always *had* managed to look better than the rest of us in her school uniform – I think her mum had hers specially made or something because it wasn't all skimpy like ours and her jumpers didn't go bobbly – but she was also really brown now (browner than Jane) and her hair, although it had grown longer, was still in an expensive-looking and shiny bob.

We all said hello and asked her how Barbados was, and she talked a bit about the wonderful weather and swimming every day and all the fantastic food, but all the time she was looking round for Philippa, who'd been her shadow the whole of last term.

We'd all reckoned that having Philippa toadying about behind her would have driven Annabel absolutely potty, but she hadn't seemed to mind. When we'd met her nasty mum at the swimming pool 'party' and then heard that she'd been brought up by housekeepers and *au pairs*, it all seemed a bit more understandable, as if Annabel just liked having someone of her own. We all thought it was a pity that it couldn't be anyone nicer than creepy Philippa, though.

Philippa came in at last – stuck close to Jane,

of course, with Cerise on the other side. I think they'd spent the entire lunch hour rubbing cream into Jane's hands.

'Hi!' Annabel said to Philippa happily, and then her eyes fell on Jane. 'Who's *this*?'

Philippa's jaw dropped and there was a moment's silence as Annabel and Jane stared at each other and weighed each other up.

Both Annabel and Jane were a bit glossy and special, a bit out-of-the-ordinary, and it was immediately quite obvious that each thought *they* should be the only glossily interesting one.

'I'm Araminta Eversage,' Jane said to her coolly. 'I expect you recognise me, don't you?'

'No,' Annabel said. 'Should I, then?'

'Well, I have been on television quite a bit. I'm in *Village Life*, for instance.'

'I never watch soaps,' Annabel said. 'Never seen you before in my life.'

'You remember . . . at the end of last term . . . we heard someone was coming . . . who was on TV,' Philippa stuttered.

'No, I don't remember at all,' Annabel said carelessly. 'Is this her?'

'Yes . . . er . . . this is Araminta. She's done adverts, too,' said Philippa miserably, absolutely torn between the two of them.

'You can call her Jane if you like,' Erica put in, 'lots of us do.'

'Yes, well, how interesting . . .' Annabel drawled, and she all but yawned. She turned her back on Jane and slung her leather school bag over her shoulder. 'Where are we sitting, Philippa? Usual seat in the corner?'

Philippa went pink. She'd moved to sit behind Cerise and Jane, of course, near the window for best view of the boys' school and as close as possible to Jane in the interests of maximum toadying.

'No . . . I'm . . . we're here next to the window,' Philippa said, moving towards their seat.

Cerise, now wearing a beaming smile at the thought of having Jane all to herself, sat herself down and Jane joined her, flouncing away from Annabel with her nose in the air.

Annabel looked at her selected place. 'Don't think much of it over here,' she said, making a face at Jane's back.

Just then Mrs Mackie came in with the register under her arm. After meeting Mrs Mackie, Mum once said that she was very shrewd: 'the sort of woman who could sum up a situation in two seconds and act upon it in three', she'd said, and right then I knew what she meant.

Mrs Mackie, knowing how Philippa had trailed after Annabel all last term, must have realised immediately that Annabel and Jane would hate each other on sight. Now, Mrs Mackie hated Jane, too, of course, even more so since the assembly business, so she immediately made a great fuss of Annabel.

'How lovely to have you back, dear!' she said, and we all made goggle eyes at each other. Mrs Mackie was only known to call

65

girls 'dear' when they were half-dead with something and on their way to nurse.

'How was Barbados? I hope you had a lovely time. You certainly look marvellous on it. Doesn't she, class?' she said, looking round at the rest of us.

'Yes, I had a lovely time, thank you,' Annabel said, looking as surprised as everyone else.

'Sit down then, dear,' Mrs Mackie said. 'Philippa, move your chair a little so that Annabel can get in.'

Everyone sat down, all trying to hide grins. Jane put her hand up. 'Yes?' Mrs Mackie snapped.

'I need to go early today,' Jane said, 'I've got a script read-through for a *Village Life* Easter special.'

'Well, I'm afraid they'll have to have it without you,' Mrs Mackie said, opening the register. 'I can't have my class going off as and when they want to. This is a proper school, where we teach proper lessons, not some Mickey Mouse stage school.'

'But I . . .'

'That's all!' said Mrs Mackie. 'I've had just about enough of you, young lady.' She banged on her desk for silence from the rest of us and began calling the afternoon register.

I saw Jane flounce and fume a bit and then, while Mrs Mackie was eyes-down over the desk, she started scribbling on a sheet of paper. When Mrs Mackie got to her name she called it out, ultra-politely, and then held up the paper so the rest of the class could see it. It said:

COMING SOON! MACKEREL FACE – THE REVENGE!

Chapter Six
MOUSE FIGHTS BACK

It was break and raining hard so we couldn't go out, and Fleur and I were starving. I'd had a Kit-Kat but I'd eaten it on the way to school, while Fleur swore she hadn't eaten at all for days.

'Not proper food, anyway,' she added mournfully.

'What not meat and two vegetables?' I asked.

'Oh, I've had *that*. Real food, I mean: chocolate, slabs of toffee, honeycomb, fruit gums, nut clusters,' she said. 'I can't remember the last time I had a decent nut cluster . . .'

'But look how nice and slim you are . . .'

'So what? I'd give it all up for a packet of marshmallows. *One* marshmallow.'

We went to look in the bottom of our lockers to see if there might be a peanut or two lurking in the dust, but there was nothing except half a stick of chewing gum, which we shared. It wasn't exactly thrilling, though, in fact a quarter of a stick of chewing gum is so small that when it's chewed up it's hardly worth moving your jaws for.

Mouse was standing by the lockers and fiddling about with her school bag. 'Got anything to eat?' I asked her. 'Any chance of lending us a crisp or two until tomorrow?'

She shook her head. 'I *did* have a nice block of fudge,' she said, 'but it went.'

'Where?' Fleur asked.

'Into Alison's pocket,' Mouse said, but in a strange voice. What I mean is, she didn't sound all that upset about it.

'Is she still taking stuff?' I asked.

'Oh, yes . . . she's been getting worse,' Mouse said quite happily.

'Right!' Fleur said. 'We'll have a good think and . . .'

'It's okay,' Mouse said. 'Honestly it is!'

We looked at her in surprise. 'Why is it?'

Mouse grinned. 'You'll see in a minute. And after this I don't think Alison will be taking things from me any more.'

'Why? Have you told someone?' I asked. 'Did you go and see Mrs Mackie?'

'No, I . . .' Mouse said, and then we heard a sudden roar of anger from Alison.

'My mouth's on fire!' she yelled. 'Water, quickly!'

Well, there wasn't any water around and

even if there *had* been, I don't think anyone would have rushed to get it.

'Help!' she said, spitting all over the floor. 'I've been poisoned!'

Alice suddenly took pity on her and ran over with the remains of a cardboard carton of orange juice.

'Quickly, drink some of this!' she said.

While we sat watching her, goggle-eyed, Alice spat into a tissue, wiped all round her mouth and gulped down the orange. 'Where's Mouse?' she croaked when she could speak.

'Here!' Mouse said meekly.

'What was in that fudge?' Alison asked. 'It was awful – I'm sure I've been poisoned!'

'I don't know exactly *what* was in it,' Mouse said, 'because you took it before I could try it, didn't you?'

Alison looked furious. 'It was like . . . like red hot peppers!' she said. 'You were trying to kill me!'

'*Did* you take it from Mouse?' Alice asked Alison severely.

Alison shrugged. 'So what if I did? I just said I was hungry and asked her what she had to eat. No crime in that, is there?' she asked aggressively.

Alice looked at her reproachfully. 'I thought you'd stopped all that after last term,' she said. 'I didn't think you'd ever start taking things again.'

Alison, still scouring her mouth out with a hanky, pretended not to hear her.

70

'Sorry you didn't like my fudge, Alison,' Mouse said quietly. 'Perhaps you'd better not have anything else from me, then.'

Alison glared at her, absolutely furious but unable to say a word.

Mouse, carrying some books, moved towards an empty desk at the front of the class. 'And, by the way, I'm moving desks,' she went on, 'I'm going to sit here on my own from now on and if Mrs Mackie asks why, I'll just say I can't hear properly.'

'Good for you!' someone called from the back of the class, and Alice added, 'Let this be a lesson to you, Alison. We'll be watching for you from now on . . .'

Alison rushed out, saying she was going to the cloakroom for some water, and we all gathered round Mouse wanting to know what she'd done.

'Well, you know I told you that my dad was an artist,' she said, 'well, he's actually a graphic designer. He designs packets and boxes for things like cornflakes and biscuits. I told him about Alison taking things from me and he said the best way of getting back at her would be to cook up a really nasty home-made bar of something and wait for her to pinch it.'

The block of fudge which Alison had dropped was still on the floor and I picked it up. 'So did your dad make this?' I asked, holding out the packet.

Mouse nodded. 'He designed the packet

on some special greaseproof paper and we painted it, and then my mum and I made the fudge between us.'

'What did it have in it?' Su asked. 'Was it really poison?'

Mouse shook her head, 'It wouldn't actually *hurt* anyone,' she said. 'It was just ordinary fudge mixture but with some of the chilli powder that my mum uses for curries.'

'Great idea!' Erica said, and we all nodded agreement and said it was brilliant.

At lunchtime it was still wet outside, but we were entertained by the sight of Jane rehearsing her extremely important part in the cat food advertisement, which was actually being filmed the next day.

Mrs Mackie had already had a go about the fact that Jane needed a day off school, and first of all she'd said she couldn't go, and had gone through all the 'This is a proper school, not a . . .' etc. etc. bit again, but then Jane had appealed to Miss Harmer, who'd agreed that she could go straight away. Anything Mrs Mackie was against, Miss Harmer was all for.

Cerise and Philippa were lined up ready to help with the rehearsal. Jane had taken the saucers from underneath the classroom pot plants and placed them on the floor at the front of the class, while we all sat on desks and craned our necks to see.

'Now, you stand behind this saucer, Cerise,' Jane commanded, 'and you, Philippa, are behind the blue one.'

Philippa and Cerise moved into place, standing obediently behind their saucers and waiting for instructions.

'Now! You, Cerise, move a little bit to the right, and then you bend down and pretend to scoop out some cat food on to your saucer from a tin,' Jane said in her bossiest voice.

'Okay,' Cerise said, and she did as instructed, all the time looking up into an imaginary camera and smiling stupidly.

'Not like that,' Jane said. 'You're not supposed to know the camera is there. You're not in a television studio, I *told* you; you're supposed to be feeding your cat in your own kitchen at home. Try and use your imagination.'

'But my cat is fed outside,' Cerise complained. 'He's half wild, you see, and Mummy says that . . .'

'Never mind that,' Jane said impatiently. 'We're not here to discuss your cat's feeding habits, we're here to help me rehearse my part. Just put the food in the saucer, then stand back and look very sad because your cat isn't eating.'

'Oh, just a sec,' Cerise said, standing up. She'd taken to wearing a pink lace bow in her hair when Mrs Mackie wasn't around, and it had slipped to one side during 'filming' and was hanging over her face. 'Must fix this. Must look nice for the cameras!'

Jane gritted her teeth. 'There aren't any cameras here, Cerise,' she said.

'Just using my imagination like you said,' Cerise said happily.

'Okay, Philippa,' Jane went on wearily, 'you now. You bend down and put your cat food out, and then *your* cat starts to eat it and then he stops and looks up at you and you say, "What's wrong, Puss?"'

'Why haven't I got any lines?' Cerise wanted to know.

'Because you'd get them wrong,' Jane said. 'Now, have you got that, Philippa?'

'What's wrong, Puss?' Philippa said in a dead pan voice. 'Is that right?'

'Well, that's not very good, is it?' Cerise said indignantly. 'I could do it better than that. Let me have a try!'

Jane sighed loudly. '*Do* try to sound as if you're really concerned as to why he's lost his appetite, Philippa. Haven't you got a cat?'

'Yes, but he's never ill,' Philippa said anxiously. 'I just don't know how I'd talk to him if . . .'

'Just use your imagination!' Jane said.

'What's wrong, Puss? What's wrong, Puss?' Philippa asked in a false and heartbroken voice, bending almost flat on the floor with the strain of forcing a poor dying cat to eat its food. 'Oh, what's wrong, Puss?' She pulled an imaginary hanky out of her pocket and wiped imaginary tears from her face.

'Yes, well, no need to overdo it,' Jane said. 'Now,' she went on, 'here comes the important bit.'

'The bit where she comes in . . .' I whispered to Fleur.

'The bit where I come in,' Jane went on. 'I'm carrying a tin of . . . well . . . I'd better just call it Pussochops because I can't reveal the correct brand name yet – it's a trade secret – and I say to both of you, "Have you tried Pussochops yet?"'

'And what do I say?' Cerise asked eagerly.

'You don't say anything,' Jane said. 'You just stay crouching by your saucers and looking up at me hopefully because I'm going to save your cat's life.'

'I just wish I had some words to say,' Cerise said plaintively. 'Can't I have Philippa's part?'

'No!' Jane said fiercely. 'Now, I'm going to scoop some of *my* cat food into clean saucers.' She removed two more plant saucers from under the plants on Mrs Mackie's desk, and said, 'There's not a cat alive who doesn't like Pussochops!'

'Is there a dead one?' I asked, and we all screeched with laughter.

Jane ignored us. 'Then your two cats run to eat out of my saucers and I say, "Pussochops! The cat food that your cat will leave home for!" And then there's a very long close-up of me holding the cat food tin up to my face and I say, "Pussochops for your contented cat!"' She paused, 'Now, I think we'll just try it all once more. From the top, as we say in the studios . . .'

'And I'll have the speaking part this time,

75

shall I?' Cerise said, kicking Philippa's saucer out of the way. 'Was I any good, Araminta? Mummy says I'd be an absolute natural on telly. I was on a video once when I was bridesmaid to my cousin. I looked really lovely, I had this . . .'

'Yes, we'll do it again, I think,' Jane said, interrupting loudly. 'Does anyone else want a go?'

Jasbir did, and Donna. They took their places behind the saucers.

'I'll be at the studios really early,' Jane said to anyone who was interested. 'I need to be in Hair and Make-up practically at dawn. They make you look absolutely wonderful, but sometimes it takes ages.'

Annabel snorted. She and Jane still hadn't taken to each other – I didn't think they ever would.

'Of course, they like my hair *au naturel*,' Jane said, ignoring the snort and tossing back about a mile of Jerry Hall-style long blonde hair. 'Some things they just can't improve on, you see.'

'Pass the sick bag . . .' Annabel said.

Chapter Seven
STOP THIEF!

'Are you looking forward to it, then?' I asked Mouse, pointing towards the skiing poster stuck up in our classroom.

She nodded. 'It should be a laugh.'

'Apparently all the teachers are completely different when they're away from the school,' I said. 'Some magic happens so that they all turn jolly and carefree.'

'*Even* Mrs Mackie?' Mouse asked.

'So they say . . .' I grinned.

We were early and Mouse had come over to my desk for a chat. Since the 'hot fudge' incident she'd managed to shake off Alison entirely. Alison, I'd decided, was really weird. She knew she'd been set up with the fudge and must have known that no one liked her, but she still carried on as normal: bossing us about (or trying to), calling everyone nasty names, hanging about where she wasn't wanted and making rude or stupid comments all the time. I couldn't understand it. Well, if it had been *me* that no one liked, I'd have tried to change. Alison couldn't seem to do anything else but be horrible, though.

Everyone started arriving in class and then Mrs Mackie appeared to take the register. After register she collected the money we brought from home every week towards our skiing trip and marked the amounts down in a book, then started reading out something about the after-school sports club.

When she'd finished Jane put up her hand. Mrs Mackie ignored her for a while – she always did that – but finally she asked, 'Yes, what is it, Jane?' in a voice which said she didn't really want to know and wasn't the slightest bit interested.

Jane stood up as if she was going to make an exciting announcement. She clasped her hands in front of her, faced sideways on so she could look both at Mrs Mackie and at us, and took a deep breath.

'I've been asked by my director on *Village Life* . . .' she began, and Mrs Mackie looked to heaven and everyone else groaned, '. . . if a camera crew can come to the school and make a special feature,' she finished.

Well, this *was* exciting. Cerise gave a little shriek and the rest of us looked at each other gleefully.

'It would be publicity for me, of course, but lots for the school, too,' Jane said. 'They want to make a short film for one of the *Newsday* programmes – something about a typical day in the life of a young actress,' she smirked.

There was a pause while we all digested this information. Okay, she was a terrible show-off and okay, most of the time she got on our nerves, but it would be quite exciting to be filmed. Tell a lie – it would be hysterically exciting to be filmed. For that even *I* would stand next to Jane and act as if I was her best friend.

'Will all of us be in it?' Cerise asked.

Jane nodded. 'The whole class.'

'And perhaps close-ups of a very special friend?' Cerise asked coyly.

'Maybe . . .' Jane said, as we all started talking about it. Well, most of us did. Annabel tried desperately not to look even slightly interested and Philippa just sat there looking uncomfortable. Since Annabel had come back she'd been absolutely torn between last term's number one heroine and *this* term's, and though I knew she'd love to be featured as a 'special friend', it was more than likely that Cerise would get *that* honour now.

Mrs Mackie clapped her hands for silence. 'Calm down, girls, please,' she said, 'and don't let's get too excited yet. I'm afraid that much as Jane would like to get lots of publicity for herself through the school, there are certain channels which much be gone through. For a start I would have to contact Miss Harmer and then the Board of Governors and then probably the Local Education Authority. They look very seriously indeed at any media attention given to the school and – who knows – they may not feel that any publicity would be good. It may put off certain parents; they may not want their daughter to attend school with an' – she gave a slight cough – 'an *actress*.'

'But, Mrs Mackie, it'd be so thrilling!' Cerise wailed. 'Oh, do let them come!'

'We'll see,' Mrs Mackie said.

'We might get other members of the cast coming as well!' Cerise screeched, as the thought of Patrick Parker on school premises suddenly struck her.

'I sincerely hope not,' Mrs Mackie said.

We had a school assembly after register and on the way to it we all clustered round Jane a bit – even I did a bit of clustering – and asked when the crew was likely to come.

'It'll all be according to their schedules,' Jane said. 'You wouldn't know unless you're actually *in* television but everything is planned for months ahead. They mentioned March 3rd – that's a Friday, and they'd want to do quite a lot of the filming after school hours because it would be quieter.'

'If I have a new perm now it should have settled down nicely by then,' Cerise said, smiling at everyone and patting her hair.

'March 3rd?' Annabel's voice came from behind us. 'That's my birthday.'

'So what?' Jane said, and added sweetly, 'please don't worry if you can't stay.'

'Well, nor can Philippa nor about ten of the others,' Annabel said. 'I'm taking them all to a dry ski slope party straight from school.' She waved over to me and Fleur, 'You two, and the twins, and Philippa and Su and Wendy and Erica. You're all invited. I was getting the invitations out this week.'

Fleur and I looked at each other. I wasn't sure whether Annabel had been going to invite everyone out or not, but it definitely was her birthday.

'What's a dry ski slope party?' Arina asked.

'Well,' Annabel said, 'it's going to be a mini-bus to the dry ski slope in Huntley, and then we'll all try out skiing for an hour and maybe have a bit of tuition, and then after that hot chocolate and hamburgers in the café.'

I was really torn. I fancied the idea of having a go on the dry ski slopes but I didn't want to miss out on the filming, either. How was I or any of us going to tell Annabel that?

Jane looked disgruntled. 'Can't you go another day?' she said. 'D'you have to go then?'

'My birthday's my birthday,' Annabel said. 'It's the day I was born. I can't change that even for someone as important as you.'

'It doesn't matter about all of them, Araminta,' Cerise said. 'I'll still be here.'

Jane shook her head, 'My producer told me he'd want to shoot all the class,' she said

81

crossly. 'It won't look very good if half is missing, will it?'

'Well, they'll have to change their date then, won't they?' Annabel said. 'That's if Mrs Mackie allows them to come at all – which I doubt.'

'Oh, she will if she knows what's good for her,' Jane said as we trooped into assembly.

No one had lost any housepoints this time but, as far as I was concerned, assembly was a nightmare.

First came the boring bits: Miss Harmer went through all the different things the after-school clubs were doing, and then spoke about skiing, and then gave a short lecture on the importance of letting young skins breathe, not clogging them up with nasty thick porridgey foundation creams that – take her word for it – young skin was far better off without.

After that she took a breath and picked up a large cardboard box which she held out in front of her.

'Lost property!' she declared. 'Unmarked lost property. Now, I believe I may have mentioned before that everything that comes into this school – and I mean *everything* – must be marked. Well, these things are not. I am going to hold them up and I want their owners to come forward and claim them.'

She started waving stuff about: it was mostly scarves and jumpers and non-school-uniform stuff which was recognised by its owners. They went up to the platform, red-faced and embarrassed, and Miss Harmer barked something at them so they went back to their seats even redder.

Almost at the bottom of the box was a disgusting-looking vest; grey-white, with a hole under each arm, and so old it was frilly round the bottom.

'This looks more like a cleaning rag than a vest,' she said, and we all laughed merrily. 'And I do believe it's a boy's. Anyone borrowed her brother's vest?'

We all laughed again – as with Mrs Mackie's jokes, it was best to laugh – but I suddenly went cold all over. At the end of last term I'd run out of vests and, because mum said it looked like snow out, she'd forced me to wear one of my eldest brother Mark's old vests. 'No one will see it,' she'd said, 'and you're positively not going out without a vest on . . .'

It *couldn't be*, could it? I felt quite sick. No, surely not. Well, even if it was, I definitely wasn't going to claim it . . . it could stay in that box for ever.

'Just a minute,' Miss Harmer said, holding the vest at arm's length. 'This *has* got a name on it. Oh, I do beg its owner's pardon; this lovely garment is marked!'

The school hooted with laughter and Miss Harmer peered at the label in the grey vest. She read out: 'M. Young,' and I went cold and then hot. She looked up, 'I expect she's missed this valuable item, so would M. Young please come and claim it.'

All the first years looked at me in surprise, and then started grinning. Fleur shot me a sympathetic look and gave me a gentle poke in the ribs. 'You'll have to get up,' she whispered.

I stood up and the whole school – it felt like the whole world – turned to stare at me.

'Ah, one of Mrs Mackie's girls!' Miss Harmer said pleasantly. 'It's surprising, isn't it, how many times her girls seem to hit the limelight . . .'

Mrs Mackie shot a venomous look at Miss Harmer, but I didn't really notice because I was concentrating on getting to the platform without tripping or treading on too many feet.

'Your vest, is it?' Miss Harmer asked when I reached her, and I shook my head.

'My brother's. I . . . er . . . borrowed it one day. It was when we were doing the Revue . . . I got changed quickly to get into my sequins and I must have forgotten it,' I stuttered.

'Ah yes, the magician's assistant with the dead rabbit! How could we forget!' Miss Harmer said, and I quickly grabbed the vest, stuffed it up my jumper and made my way back.

At lunchtime I borrowed some scissors and cut it into a million pieces. I *hated* Miss Harmer . . .

Jane talked a lot about the film at lunchtime. It almost beat my vest for Interesting Things to Talk About, but I don't know whether Mrs Mackie asked permission for the camera crew to come that day, because later something happened which pushed it out of everyone's minds.

We'd just finished our last lesson and had gone back to the classroom for our coats and bags when Mrs Mackie came striding in and went straight to her desk.

'See you tomorrow, girls,' she said as everyone started drifting out. 'Have a nice evening.'

'Not with the amount of homework *I've* got,' Fleur said gloomily, and then, just as she and I reached the door, Mrs Mackie gave a strange sort of shout. 'Oh, no!' she said, and when we looked round she had her hand to her mouth and was staring in the desk.

'What is it, Mrs Mackie?' Alice asked. She was usually on hand for emergencies.

'Nothing . . . nothing . . .' Mrs Mackie said in a distracted voice. 'It must be here somewhere.'

She started scrabbling around in her desk drawer, and then began taking the books and papers out one by one and putting them on the floor systematically. 'It must be here . . . it was here this morning,' she said almost to herself.

'Can I help you?' Alice asked. 'What is it you're looking for?'

Mrs Mackie shook her head, staring in the now-empty drawer. 'It's definitely not here,' she said almost to herself.

'Is it the register you've lost, or . . . or what?' Alice asked.

Mrs Mackie looked at her and sighed. 'Well, you'll all have to know,' she said. 'I'm very much afraid that it's the skiing money. I had it this morning, and now it's disappeared.'

We all made alarmed faces at each other.

'Are you sure?' Fleur said.

'Maybe you took it to the secretary,' I suggested.

'I should have done,' Mrs Mackie said. 'I should have taken it to Mrs Green straight after register this morning, but because I was pressed for time I just left it here. At lunch time I was helping with the music club and I forgot all about it.'

'Was the drawer locked?' Alice asked.

Mrs Mackie shook her head. 'I'm afraid not. I should have locked it, in fact I thought I did, but the turning mechanism doesn't always work, and it obviously didn't this morning.'

Those of us still left in the room stood around looking at each other and not knowing what to say.

Mrs Mackie seemed to collect herself. 'Alice, go outside and get the rest of the class back in,' she said. 'You'll have to tell them what's happened and, as this is an emergency, you'll have to be prepared to miss your buses tonight.'

'Right, Mrs Mackie,' Alice said, and went off looking shaken.

'The rest of you sit down, please,' Mrs Mackie said, 'while I think what to do for the best.'

A few minutes later Alice came back in

again. There were a few girls who had already gone home by car or on foot but she'd managed to get everyone else, and they came in looking half-excited and half-alarmed and went to their normal seats.

Mrs Mackie sat out at the front with the skiing register in front of her. 'Now,' she said, 'as you know, I collect £10 from the skiing girls every Friday. Some of the money was paid by cheque and some in cash. I want everyone who paid cash to put up their hands.'

I put mine up, and five other girls did as well. The rest had given Mrs Mackie a cheque or, in Annabel's case, had paid the full amount already.

'That's sixty pounds,' Mrs Mackie said in a worried voice. 'Sixty pounds cash. The missing cheques aren't so important; they can be replaced.'

Philippa put up her hand. 'Will we lose that ten pounds?' she asked in a whiney voice.

'I shouldn't think so, Philippa,' Mrs Mackie said. 'The school will probably be covered by insurance.' She paused, 'This is a police matter, though,' she said, 'and that's why I'm giving the thief the opportunity to come clean.'

We all shifted uncomfortably in our seats and I felt myself go all hot and cold with guilt, just as I had in assembly that morning. I wondered if I could possibly have taken the money by mistake, taken it and then had an instant loss of memory. Maybe it was in my school bag and I didn't know it . . .

'A police matter,' Mrs Mackie repeated, 'that's why I'm not saying anything to Miss Harmer or anyone else yet. At present this is strictly between ourselves – understand?'

We all nodded.

'I'm going to give the thief a chance to replace the money,' Mrs Mackie went on. 'Now, the cheques and the cash were in an envelope like this one . . .' She held up a creased brown envelope with Park Wood Girls' School printed on it. 'I want you all to search around now and tomorrow morning, and see if you can find it. I feel that thief may have an attack of conscience, feel guilty about what she's done and leave the envelope somewhere.'

Erica put up her hand. 'Mrs Mackie – it may not be someone in this class who's taken it,' she said.

'No, it may not, Erica,' Mrs Mackie said. 'But I've only taken two classes in here today, and both times I've been present before the girls arrived and after they left. You, though, my own class, have been in here before school and at breaks and lunchtimes and so on and in each case you've been unsupervised.' She raised her eyebrows, 'And everyone here, of course, knew that I'd collected the skiing money this morning.'

We all started talking at once, trying to remember who'd been in the classroom and when.

'Of course Mackerel-face doesn't want Miss Harmer to know,' I heard Jane say in a low voice, 'she realises she'd get into trouble for leaving the money in there and the drawer unlocked.'

'Who d'you think it is?' Fleur asked in a whisper.

'Must be Alison,' I whispered back

'I blame myself, of course, for not double-checking that the drawer was locked,' Mrs Mackie said. 'One doesn't imagine that this sort of thing can ever happen, though, it's absolutely shocking.' She looked almost tearful. 'Oh dear, oh dear – nothing like this ever happened with my last lot of first years,' she added.

Chapter Eight
ULTIMATUM

The following morning, before register, we gathered in excited little groups.

'It has to be one of our year,' Erica said. 'Stands to reason. It's only us who knows that Mrs Mackie collected the skiing money yesterday.'

'And only us who knew that she'd put the money in her desk – a desk which doesn't lock properly!' Annabel said.

'It must have been Alison!' I said, after looking round to make sure she wasn't about. 'We all know she pinches things – this is just one step on from bars of chocolate and blocks of fudge.'

'We mustn't accuse anyone yet!' Alice warned. 'We've got to do what Mrs Mackie said – have a good old search around. The person who took it wouldn't want the police in, would she? She's bound to get scared and put it back.'

'Old Mackerel-face only said she'd give us a day to find the money so she could put off reporting the theft to Miss Harmer,' Jane said scornfully. 'She knows she's going to get into serious trouble when she does – she might even get the sack.'

'What, because one of her class has pinched some money?' I asked.

'No, because she didn't take the money to the secretary,' Jane said. 'Stupid woman! I bet she hasn't asked Miss Harmer about the film crew coming, either. My producer rang me last night specially to find out about it.'

But no one was actually paying much attention to the film right then.

'I don't know what we'll do if the money isn't found,' Jasbir suddenly said dolefully. 'Arina and I brought ten pounds cash each and our mum won't be able to pay it again.'

'Mrs Mackie said there'd be insurance,' I said, 'but if there isn't won't your dad pay?'

Jasbir's lower lip quivered. 'He doesn't know we're going!' she said.

We all stared at the twins in surprise.

'You know he's really strict,' Arina explained, 'we just never quite got around to telling him, that's all.'

'He'll have to know some time, though,' Fleur said. 'What about when you suddenly appear in multi-coloured salopettes with your suitcases in your hands, you won't be able to say you're just popping out to the library, will you?'

'We are going to tell him,' Arina said, 'we just haven't got round to it. Mum really wanted us to go, you see, so she told us to put our names down first and worry about it afterwards. It was really quite a thing for her to be so daring,' she added.

'But if the first he hears of it is from school that the money's disappeared . . .' Jasbir said in the choked voice that meant she was going to cry, 'he'll start saying that it's all badly organised and everything and we won't be able to go.'

'Oh, don't start crying again,' Arina said in a bored voice. 'We might find the money yet.'

'Shall we start looking now?' Erica said. 'Let's go through Alison's desk before she gets here.'

'No, we'd better not,' Alice said. 'We'll organise it properly. At lunchtime we'll have a desk each and go through them looking for clues.'

'I'll do Alison's!' I said. Well, it *had* to be her . . .

Mrs Mackie came in with the register and called us all to attention.

'I'm not going to say anything about yesterday's occurrence,' she said, 'at the moment, I'm just going to pretend that it hasn't happened. You have one whole day, girls, to try and put things right. If the envelope is found and replaced in my desk by four o'clock this afternoon, no more need be said. Alternatively, if whoever took the money would like to come and see me privately, no one else need know about it.'

We all wriggled uncomfortably as she went on, 'The only other option, as you know, is to bring in the police, so if the culprit hasn't been found by this afternoon, I will inform Miss Harmer and the police will be called.' She cleared her throat. 'I will now call the register.'

After a very solemn register with no interuptions we all started making our way towards the science lab.

'Of course, she's done it all wrong again,' Jane said as we walked along the corridor. 'She should have carried out body searches last night before we left. It's not much good us all looking round now, is it? I expect that whoever took the money has got it at home somewhere.'

'Not necessarily,' Alice said. 'Whoever took it could have expected that the class would be searched and so hidden it somewhere in school.'

'That's true,' Su said. 'And anyway, I don't think Mrs Mackie would be allowed to body search anyone. Don't you have to have police present? They always do on the telly.'

Our science lesson passed off without incident except that Jasbir turned up the bunsen burner just as Arina was bending over the bench so Arina's topknot of hair and a few wispy bits of her fringe got singed.

We all waited for Arina to leap on Jasbir from a great height, but instead, strangely, she was pleased. 'I've wanted my hair cut for ages but my dad wouldn't let me,' she explained. 'Now I can make it a bit worse and then tell him I'll have to have it short.'

'Well, don't tell him it was me who burnt it!' Jasbir squeaked.

We all ate a very quick lunch – no one went home today – and then returned to our classroom. I don't know if Mrs Mackie had told anyone else what was going on, but we shut the door and no one bothered us or tried to make us go outside in the playground.

'What we've got to do is all take a desk – not our own, of course,' Alice said, 'and go through it book by book and paper by paper.'

'But it's a complete waste of time!' Jane said. 'I told you whoever took it has got the money at home now!'

'I don't think they have,' Alice said. 'Anyway, we told Mrs Mackie we'd search for it and that's what we're going to do. After we've looked in the desks we'll go through Mrs Mackie's drawer again, and then the cupboards and the waste bin and behind the radiators and any other place where an envelope or the money could be hidden.'

Alice was the unofficial prefect of the class, the first years didn't have real prefects, and everyone obeyed her. It was all deadly serious stuff. We each got assigned a desk – I didn't get Alison's, though – and began turning it out. I didn't really think anyone was going to find anything, but I watched anxiously as Su went through my desk, just in case it turned out that I'd taken the money in my sleep or something . . .

We were all busy searching when there was a sudden cry from the front of the room and Lorna, who'd been given Alice's desk to search, gave a shout.

'I've got it!' she said. 'I've found the money!'

We all stopped what we were doing and there was complete and utter silence as we all stared at her.

'In *Alice's* desk?' Erica asked in disbelief. 'You've found the money in *Alice's* desk?'

Alice had gone deathly white. 'It can't have been in there!' she said.

Lorna looked stunned. 'It was right on the top, Alice, honestly. Still in the envelope.' She shrugged helplessly. 'I just looked and there it was. It's all there – count it.'

It was passed round. It was all there – and the cheques, too.

'I didn't . . .' Alice began, and then she burst into tears. After a moment Jasbir started crying as well.

'We'd better go and get a teacher,' Philippa said.

'No!' Fleur said. 'Mrs Mackie said we should deal with it on our own and if we put the money back there'd be no questions asked.

We don't want it all round the school, do we?'

'But Alice is a thief!' Philippa said. 'It's quite obvious.' She sniffed, 'We shouldn't have to go to school with thieves.'

'I'm *not* a thief!' Alice sobbed.

'Of course she isn't,' I said. 'It isn't likely that she'd make us all hunt through each other's desks if she'd got the money right on the top of hers, is it?'

Everyone shook their heads.

'So someone else has planted it!' Fleur announced.

'All the more reason to get a teacher in,' Philippa said. 'I'm going to fetch Mrs Mackie!'

Everyone pulled her back but now Alice was no longer in charge, no one knew what to do. We just stood round in confusion shaking our heads and saying that we'd never seen the envelope before in our lives.

While we were all still standing there, the bell for the end of lunch time went and Jane suddenly walked to the front of the class and banged on Mrs Mackie's desk very loudly to shut everyone up.

She spoke in a perfectly matter-of-fact sort of voice: 'I took the money.'

There was complete silence and everyone just gaped at her.

'Of course, I didn't take it because I wanted the money,' she said scornfully. 'I took it to get Mackerel-face into trouble. Stupid old bat!'

'What d'you mean?' Erica asked.

'I took it so that Miss Harmer would realise what a useless teacher she is! I was going to wait until she had to tell Miss Harmer and *then* return the money, but all this fuss started and I thought I'd better get it back in a hurry, so I came in at break and just stuffed it into any old desk. I didn't even realise it was Alice's.'

As we all looked at each other in surprise and disbelief, Jane added, 'She's been horrible to me from the first day I got here!'

No one said anything for a minute; the only sounds were Jasbir sniffing and Alice blowing her nose.

'What do we do now, then?' I asked. 'Mrs Mackie will be in to take register in a minute.'

'Don't let's do anything.' Alice said, drying her eyes. 'I really don't care about what Jane did or why she did it – all I care about is everyone knowing that I didn't take that money.'

'So we'll just give it back to Mrs Mackie, shall we?' Fleur asked.

'I don't think we ought to do that,' Alison said nastily. 'I think we ought to tell that it was *her* . . .' and she jabbed a finger towards Jane.

'Why? We didn't tell her it was you who took all those things from us last term,' Fleur said.

'And I didn't tell her it was you who took stuff from me *this* term,' Mouse called from the back of the class.

'Let's just forget it,' Alice said. 'As far as revenges go it was a bit over the top, but I won't say anything about it if no one else does.'

'Suppose Mrs Mackie had lost her job, though?' Laura asked.

Jane flushed, 'I didn't think . . .' she muttered.

'Well, she didn't lose her job and we've got the money back so there's no harm done,' Erica said. 'I think we just ought to forget about it.'

Jane was trying to be blustery and uncaring but she was pink in the face and you could tell she was relieved to have got off so easily. 'Okay, then,' she muttered, 'I suppose it was pretty stupid of me to involve other people.'

'Who's going to give it back to Mrs Mackie?' I asked. 'She's bound to realise that whoever hands it back was involved in some way.'

'She's got to give it back – Jane has!' someone called, and a few other voices rose in agreement.

The envelope was handed over to her. 'It's your punishment,' Erica said. 'See how well you can act in *this* little scene.'

It was all over within a minute. Mrs Mackie came in, Jane went straight up to her with the money and said that it had been found, and Mrs Mackie, far from noticing who was giving it, was so overjoyed to get it back that if it had been anyone other than Jane handing it over, I think she would have kissed her.

I thought that was the end of it and it was, really, because no one else in the school found out, but that afternoon, when school had finished, I was trying to sort out my locker (Mrs Mackie had asked me if I intended to hold a jumble sale in it) and somehow missed my bus. I went into the loo to see if I could find anyone who would lend me ten pence to ring Mum, and found Jane in there crying. And not acting-crying, either.

'What's up?' I asked awkwardly, after wondering if I should just make a bolt for it.

'Nothing,' she said in a forlorn voice, bent right over the basin so that I couldn't see her face.

'There is really, isn't there?' I said, feeling that at least I ought to try. 'What's up, Jane?'

I thought she might jump on me from a great height for calling her that, but she just gave a great big sniff and said, 'No one likes me,' in a wobbly voice.

I stared at her – or what I could see of her through the curtain of hair. 'Of course they do,' I said. 'Loads of people like you . . . hundreds of people.' I thought of the television audience of *Village Life*. 'Millions, I expect.'

'I mean everyone at school,' she said, lips quivering. 'I've been really stupid – taking that money – and I nearly got Alice into trouble and caused all that fuss.' She looked at me mournfully through the hair. 'I bet everyone hates me now.'

'I bet they don't,' I said. 'It was quite exciting; cheered up a boring old day.'

'You all just want to get rid of me . . .' she went on, burying her face in her hands.

'Course we don't! If you leave we won't get on telly, will we?' I said, and then hastily added, 'And not just that. I mean, it's really interesting having you around.'

'Is it really?' she sniffed.

I nodded. She didn't look much like a star now, her nose was bright red and her eyes were all puffy.

'Because even if I wanted to leave, my mum and dad wouldn't let me go back to drama school.'

'Good!' I said.

'D'you mean that?' she asked.

'Course! We like having you here. It makes things exciting.'

She nodded, satisfied, then shook out her hair and stared at herself in the mirror. 'I still hate Mrs Mackie, though.'

I shrugged. 'She's not that awful. I know she's got it in for you, but on the whole she's not a bad old stick.'

I don't think Jane heard. She carried on staring at herself, and then her face suddenly crumpled. 'Oh, no!' she said in a heart-rending voice.

'What?'

'A spot! The most enormous spot on my nose!' She pointed dramatically. 'Look! Huge! Like a molehill . . .'

I looked; I couldn't see a thing.

'I shall fail the Golden and Delicious Corn-flakes audition!'

'Of course you won't!' I said, trying not to giggle.

'I will!'

'Bet you don't,' I said, 'they'll just take one look at you and sign you up straight away. Soon as they set eyes on you!' I wiped a hand across my forehead – talk about hard work. 'And by the way, can you lend me ten pence?'

Chapter Nine
DORIS PULLS IT OFF

'It was so funny!' I said to Mouse as we lined up ready to run up the wallbars during PE. 'I couldn't even stand! Everytime I managed to sort my legs out and get the skis straight, my feet just sort-of slid out at different angles and I was back on the ground again.'

The night before had been the dry-ski party, which everyone agreed had been more of a sore-botty party. The only ones who'd actually managed to get up on their skis and do anything had been the ones who'd been skiing before: Annabel and Su.

'Perhaps it's easier on real snow,' Mouse puffed, as Miss Hermitage made us run up the bars. She was my partner because Fleur had gone to the dentist.

'The ski instructor kept telling us that,' I said, 'but no one believed him.'

'So did you learn anything?' she asked as we hung on the top bar with our hands. 'Did you go on that big pull-up trolley thing?'

I shook my head. 'Unless you can actually stand up and do what's called a snow-plough, you're not allowed on the dry slope proper. We were only there for an hour and we spent most of that on a little practice slope trying to stand up.'

We climbed down the bars and made our way to the horse. Every part of me was aching after the night before – all the pre-skiing exercises we'd been doing for weeks didn't seem to have done me any good at all.

'Maybe everyone should go to the dry slope a few times before we go to France, we don't want to waste a whole week falling over, do we?' Mouse said.

'I don't think it'll make any difference to me,' I said, 'I don't think I'm going to be able to do it however much practice I get.'

'What about Annabel?'

'She was great, I said. 'She and Su were either skiing around us laughing all the time or whizzing up the slope on the pulley and coming down at about a hundred miles an hour.'

'So if they can do it, everyone else will be able to.'

'I bet I can't. I bet I'm the only one who'll still be a complete dope at it at the end of the week,' I said gloomily.

We jumped over the horse and then Miss Hermitage divided us up and started us on circuits around the gym.

'Will I be able to share a room with you and Fleur when we go skiing?' Mouse asked.

'From what I can make out everyone's sharing with everyone else,' I said. 'It seems to be twelve to a room.'

'Ooh good, it'll be midnight feasts and things then, will it?' Mouse asked.

'Doubt it,' I said. 'In my case it'll probably be midnight binding up of broken legs.'

Mouse was much better since she'd got rid of Alison; she spoke up in class occasionally now and had even been known to make the odd joke or two. We were all getting quite excited about skiing, though I wasn't quite so excited since I'd found out how useless I was. The twins' dad had been told about the skiing trip at last after one of the teachers had written him a special letter saying how much it would help the twins with their French, and Arina had given the letter to him and talked him round.

Fleur came in just after lunch while we were all still in the playground – her mum had taken her to McDonalds for her lunch for a special treat.

'And we went back home after and I started watching that Australian soap and . . . guess who I saw in the break?'

'Who?'

'Jane! Doing the cat food advertisement! It

104

was really funny seeing her . . . and seeing the advert actually on real telly after all the times we'd seen it rehearsed. I knew all the words – *I* could have done it!'

'What did she look like? Really pretty?'

'Quite good,' Fleur said grudgingly. She was wearing a denim jacket and the cat she picks up at the end – when she says the "for your contented cat" bit – is one of those long-haired Persian cats in the same sort of blue colour, and Jane's blonde hair flows over her shoulders and over the cat.'

'She can't know the advert's on yet,' I said. 'We would have heard about it.'

'That's what I thought,' Fleur said.

'What d'you think's going to happen about the film crew coming? Has she said anything else to Mrs Mackie?'

I shook my head. 'I don't think so. She's been a bit subdued since the skiing money thing, hasn't she?'

'Jane? Subdued?' Fleur screeched. 'Do you call being collected from school in a chauffeur-driven car subdued? Or distributing signed photographs to the dinner ladies? Or standing by the gate of the boys' school giving out autographs?'

I laughed. 'Well, subdued for *her*.' I hadn't told Fleur about the scene in the cloakroom.

We were sitting around in class waiting for Mrs Mackie to come in and take afternoon register when Philippa, who'd been keeping watch at the door, gave a scream.

'Miss Harmer's coming!' she yelled. 'Quickly, everyone!'

We just about had time to tie our hair back, pull up our socks, straighten our blouses and sit up straight before Miss Harmer walked through the door with our register under her arm.

She cast a beady eye over us. 'Mrs Mackie has gone to a meeting,' she said, 'so I've come to take register this afternoon.'

She put the book down on the desk and began walking up and down the aisles inspecting us. She had an itchy tweedy skirt and a horrible nylon blouse with a bit of lace around the collar, so she didn't exactly look like a *Vogue* model, but every now and then she'd seize on a bitten set of fingernails, find a smudge on someone's collar or point at a greasy spot on someone's skirt and say, 'This is nothing to be proud of, is it?' and whoever it was would have to look ashamed of themselves and murmur that no, it wasn't. Then she'd murmur something like, 'Hm . . . well, what does one expect from Mrs Mackie's class?' under her breath.

As Jane and Cerise sat near the window she got to them nearly last, and by this time they'd managed to wipe off their pink lipstick, flatten and pull back their hair and pull down their skirts so that they looked fairly normal.

Miss Harmer smiled warmly at Jane, or as warmly as her smiles ever got. Since the housepoint assembly, when she'd realised that

106

Mrs Mackie hated Jane, she'd gone out of her way to be nice to her, and if we ever saw Miss Harmer round the school she'd just glower at everyone else but stop Jane to say a few smarmy words. I think she was hoping for a walk-on part in *Village Life*. The village witch, maybe.

'Ah, our little star!' she said now, reaching her desk. 'Settling down all right, are you?'

'Yes, thank you,' Jane said demurely.

'It's always difficult when you start at school a term later than everyone else.'

'Yes, Miss Harmer,' Jane said. 'Er . . . I wonder if I could possibly ask you something.'

'Of course,' Miss Harmer said graciously. 'I like to think my girls can always come to me with their problems.' She smiled coyly. 'Even though I may look old, my dear, I can still remember what it's like to be young. Never feel there is anything you cannot confide in me.'

'It's not exactly a problem,' Jane said, 'it's just . . . well, my producer asked me if they could make a short film at school. A general interest one – a day in the life of a TV star, you know? For *Newsday*.'

'I see,' Miss Harmer said, while we all sat perfectly still and staring at the front, just our ears waggling.

'I did ask Mrs Mackie once but she seems to have forgotten about it,' Jane said plaintively. 'And although it would benefit me, of course, I was also thinking how lovely it would be for the other girls.' She looked all round the room, beaming a loving and generous smile in all directions. 'You see, some of them may not get another chance to be on television.

'The film unit would come at the end of term so they wouldn't disrupt things too much,' she went on earnestly, 'and it would be marvellous publicity for the school. *Newsday* goes out at four-thirty so millions of people would see it ... and it would be all about what a wonderful school it was and how happy I am here.'

I nudged Fleur hard, because Jane was always going on about what rubbish she was taught here, how the teachers were useless and how she didn't know how Park Wood could even *call* itself a school ...

'Well, what a perfectly lovely idea!' Miss Harmer said. 'I'm sure the governors would have no objection – I'll speak to them this afternoon. Lots of publicity for the school, you say?'

Jane nodded. 'All about what a marvellous school this is.'

'Wonderful ... wonderful.' Miss Harmer said, and then frowned, 'I can't understand why Mrs Mackie didn't let me know about this straight away. It is most lax of her.' Her tight lips went into another smile. 'You tell your producer to ring me to arrange the date, and I'll put whatever facilities they need at their disposal. No turn shall be unturned! Park Wood shall have its day!'

'Yes, Miss Harmer,' Jane said, looking a little

taken-aback at this gush of girlish enthusiasm from the woman she referred to as the old trout.

Things started moving quickly. Miss Harmer must have spoken to the governors and the producer must have rung, because a few days later the following message was pinned up all over the school on every noticeboard:

> Will all teachers kindly ensure that pupils wear school uniform at all times and do not deviate from this under *any circumstances* (underlined twice). Our school will be under scrutiny from the media soon and standards must be rigorously upheld.

On the notice, which was pinned outside the dining hall, someone – it must have been a sixth former because no one else would have dared – had added in red pen: *On penalty of death, signed D. Harmer*, and a skull and crossbones had been drawn. Laura, who had a sister in the fifth, was despatched to find out what the 'D' stood for, and came back and told us – Doris. We all thought this was so funny that we called Miss Harmer nothing but Doris after that.

A couple of days after that, all the teachers started getting memos. In the first one they were asked to go on voluntary playground control 'to ensure the girls are playing nicely at all times' and then came another one to say that a display of the best work from every class was to be put up in the entrance hall, and the teachers were to stay behind to mount and display a 'quality arrangement'. We knew just what the memos said because when Mrs Mackie received them, fire seemed to come out of her nostrils. 'Cheap publicity stunt . . . don't know what this school is coming to,' she'd mutter, and then she'd screw them up and toss them over her shoulder into the wastebin, from where they were later retrieved and read aloud to the class by Philippa.

In the meantime, Jane kept us going with stories about the film crew.

'It'll be an Outside Broadcast team, of course,' she said, 'so I may not know all the guys who come along.' She flicked a wad of hair back, 'I just hope Danny's there . . . he's absolutely gorgeous . . .'

'Oooh,' Cerise breathed, hanging on her every word. 'Can't wait to see *him* . . .'

Philippa was hanging on her every word, too – but trying to do it in such a way that Annabel wouldn't notice and say something sarcastic.

'They may come with a mobile canteen,' Jane went on airily, 'but anyway there'll be miles and miles of cable all over the place and masses of equipment. You wouldn't believe the equipment necessary for just one little ten-minute programme!'

'Will we all have make-up?' Su wanted to know.

'No, only *I* will have the make-up,' Jane said. 'That'll be Loretta – she always does me.

Absolute sweetie, she is. Oh!' she suddenly looked aghast. 'I just hope they've remembered to get Luigi for my hair – he gets so booked up!'

I nudged Fleur hard. 'Who's doing your hair and make-up?' I asked.

She thought for a bit. 'I could ask my mum to cut my fringe,' she said. 'What about you?'

'Oh, I'm definitely having Luigi,' I said. 'Who else is there?'

A few days before the crew were due to arrive the school had been scrubbed, polished and painted to within an inch of its life. Loads of new plants had appeared in the gardens, the back fence had been done over with smelly brown stuff and the paintwork on the school building was now sea-green instead of murky grey. Teachers had been urged to wear suits to teach in (no trousers) and – so the library would appear well-stocked – everyone had to return what books they had and not take out any more until after the crew had gone.

'It's getting ridiculous,' I said to Fleur when we were wandering down the corridors on our way to art. 'I've heard now that the bike sheds have got to be painted and apparently she only wants new bikes in them. I mean, the film crew's not going to be poking around bike sheds! They only want to film their darling Araminta.'

As we tiptoed past Doris's office, she suddenly came out. Her eyes fell on me. 'Ah, the girl with the vest,' she said, 'you're a first year, aren't you?'

I nodded, wishing I hadn't let Cerise try out a new plum lipstick on me at lunch time and praying that no trace remained.

'Take this to Mrs Mackie, will you? And say that I expect her to act upon it immediately. Immediately, mind!'

She shoved a note at me and went back in her office, then poked her head out again.

'And I don't want any excuses from her! Tell her that, will you!'

Fleur and I started walking again. 'Crumbs,' Fleur said in an undertone.

'I can't tell her *that*!' I said. 'She'd kill me alive.'

'Just leave the note and run,' Fleur suggested.

'Wonder what it says?'

We looked at each other. 'Suppose I was to drop it on the floor and it sort-of unfolded,' I said slowly. 'And you picked it up and it came more unfolded . . .'

'. . . so that we just couldn't help reading it,' she finished. I dropped it on the floor and, with quite a bit of help, it came open.

'Mrs Mackie – your room is a disgrace!' I read out to Fleur. 'As the main focus of attention will be on Jane's own class I must insist that you replace the torn posters, tidy the bookshelves, give the paintwork a good wipe over and supply some livelier plants, signed, D. Harmer.'

'Oh wow!' Fleur said.

'Doris has really gone and done it now!' I said, folding the note up again. 'Mrs Mackie will hit the roof!'

'Suppose she has a fit and goes to the governors or someone and stops the whole thing?' I said.

'My mum's bought a video specially . . .' Fleur said.

'My auntie in Wales was looking forward to seeing me . . .' I said. 'What shall we do? If we don't give her the note the class won't get tidied up and Doris will go mad . . .'

'And if we *do*, Mrs Mackie will go mad.'

'What if we keep the note and do it ourselves?' I said to Fleur.

'Clean up?'

I nodded. 'Doris won't know – she'll just think that Mrs Mackie has followed her instructions. We could easily repair the posters and tidy the books.'

'And we've got some decent plants at home!'

'Mrs Mackie will just think we're being helpful.'

'So what shall we do with the note?' Fleur asked.

'How about if it unfortunately got accidentally torn into two hundred pieces?' I said, accidentally tearing it into two hundred pieces . . .

Chapter Ten
STARS FOR THE DAY

Fleur and I walked across the playground together.

'That's a very bright jumper,' I said to her.

'So is yours!'

'New?'

We both nodded resignedly.

'My mum insisted. She said that if I was going to be on television from coast to coast, at least I should have a nice new jumper,' Fleur said.

'I'm nice and new from the skin outwards,' I said. 'I even had to have my hair rolled under at the ends this morning.'

We walked across the playground towards school – towards a scrubbed, glistening, transformed school, all ready for the television cameras. As we turned the corner, one of the twins ran into us. A twin in a bright new jumper.

'Arina!' I said. 'Where're you off to in such a rush?'

'Oh . . . er . . . getting away from Jasbir!' she said, and then she burst out laughing and ran straight past us into school.

While we were staring after her, wondering what was up, the other twin appeared. At least, we thought it was a twin, except that instead of having Jasbir's long plaits, she had a short, stylish haircut – curly on the top and very short and cropped straight across the back.

'Jasbir?' Fleur and I said in amazement, and Lorna and Su, (more new jumpers) getting off another bus, came and joined us in staring at this strange twin.

'No, of course I'm not Jasbir!' the girl said crossly. 'Do I look like Jasbir? Don't you know us apart?'

'Arina?' we said.

'Of course I'm Arina!'

'But . . . Jasbir just ran past us with her hair in a bun like you have yours.'

'Like I *used* to have mine,' she said grimly.

'What happened, then?'

She puffed out her cheeks crossly. 'Well, last night my dear sister decided that she, too, would have her hair up from now on. She reckoned it would suit her better and she also wanted us to look exactly the same for the film today. I went mad, of course, and decided that the only thing to do was to get mine cut, so I went round to my mum's friend and got it all chopped off!'

We all made admiring noises. 'It looks really good,' Fleur said. 'What did your dad say, though?'

'Oh, he only went a bit mad,' Arina said carelessly. 'I had a good excuse, see. You know it got burnt the other week? Well, when I got home I just ruined it a bit more. I said there'd been another little accident in the lab and unless he wanted me to look completely revolting on television, he'd have to let me have it short.'

'So what did Jasbir do then?' Lorna asked.

'Well, she was so cross that I had short hair and she hadn't, that she decided she'd get into school early, with her hair up and looking like me, and do all sorts of stupid things so I'd get the blame.'

'But when they see you with your hair short they'll know it wasn't you!' I said.

'I told her that,' Arina said wearily, 'but you know what she's like when she gets an idea in her head.' She started off towards school again. 'If I don't stop her, though, she'll get into trouble and get us split up again and I don't want to go in another class today and miss my chance to be famous, do I?'

Su giggled as the rest of us followed Arina in. 'My dad's closing the shop the day that the film is on,' she said, 'and he's making three copies of the video to send to Hong Kong.'

'When will it be on?' I asked. 'Does anyone know?'

Su shook her head. 'I tried to ask Araminta but she went on and on about editing and cutting and how difficult it was for an ordinary person to understand these technical things.'

'That's it!' Fleur said. 'I bet I end up cut right out of it!'

'I hope they don't show it when we're away skiing,' I said.

Arina and Jasbir were still talking heatedly when we got to our class, but when Mrs Mackie came in to take the register and made it obvious that she had the hump, they went quiet.

No one needed to ask *why* she had the hump. We all knew it was because the film crew was coming.

'Mrs Mackie! We've got a new girl!' Cerise said, putting up her hand before register.

'Of course we haven't,' Mrs Mackie said. 'Don't be so silly.'

She suddenly looked round the classroom. 'The whole place is going silly – the whole school! – I see that someone's even been employed to clean up my class ... what an absolutely ridiculous waste of time and money.'

Fleur and I nudged each other. We'd done the classroom up gradually, bit by bit. The borrowed plants had come in last; Fleur's mum had brought them up in the car the day before.

Mrs Mackie looked back at Cerise. 'What are those things stuck to your eyes?' she asked.

Cerise fluttered her eyes at everyone. 'False eyelashes!' she said proudly. 'For the close-ups!'

'Straight to the cloakroom and off immediately!' Mrs Mackie said. 'I'm not having any of that nonsense in my class!'

'Oh, but Mrs Mackie . . . I'm having some close-ups taken with Araminta . . . as her special friend,' Cerise whined, 'and mummy says eyes always look smaller in photographs and they need false lashes on them.'

'Does mummy really?' said Mrs Mackie in her dangerous tone of voice, 'how very interesting.'

'Yes,' Cerise went on regardless, 'she says nature often needs a helping hand. You could do a lot with your eyes, you know, Mrs Mackie. Do you want me to make them up for you later? I've got my big beauty box with hundreds of . . .'

'Go!' Mrs Mackie thundered. 'And don't come back until you look more like a schoolgirl and less like a tart!'

Cerise scuttled out. On the back of her head she wore a pink satin bow with long streamers, and they flew out behind as she ran.

'And get that stupid bow off your hair!' Mrs Mackie roared after her.

'Disruptions . . . disruptions . . . nothing but chaos,' Mrs Mackie said, crashing things around on her desk. 'How a person is supposed to get any teaching done is beyond me.' She glowered at Jane (who looked a bit browner and a bit blonder than usual); 'I shall be glad when this whole business is over. I never heard anything so ridiculous in my life . . . a film crew coming! How anyone is supposed to teach the curriculum and instil discipline into you girls, I don't know.'

We all sat quiet as mice, waiting for Mrs Mackie to go up in flames.

'Please, Mrs Mackie . . . ' Erica said after a moment.

She'd just been about to start the register again but she looked up and sighed. 'Yes, Erica?'

'When Cerise said we had a new girl, she meant Arina!'

Mrs Mackie's eyes slid round the class. 'What are you talking about?' she said. 'Has everyone gone quite silly today?' She pointed as Jasbir, 'There's Arina. What d'you mean, she's a new girl?'

Arina, sitting next to Jasbir with a broad smile on her face, put her hand up. 'No, I'm here!' she said.

Mrs Mackie looked from one twin to the other, did a double take, and actually started to laugh. We all joined in, though what we were all shrieking about was Cerise having the nerve to offer to glamorize Mrs Mackie.

'Well, very nice you look too, Arina,' Mrs Mackie said eventually, 'and how convenient when it comes to hairwashing night! Yes . . . you look quite grown up.'

'Well, I'm getting mine cut as well . . .' we all heard Jasbir mutter rebelliously.

The film unit weren't supposed to arrive until after three o'clock, and we all felt we'd die of impatience before then. Jane was funny as she didn't know whether to be bossy and gloating towards us, or act very casual about it all, so most of the time she see-sawed between two poses. I liked her better since I'd found her crying in the loo. Sometimes, just occasionally, she seemed perfectly normal and you could almost forget she was a star.

At lunch time we put on as much mascara as we thought we could get away with and posed ourselves around the school asking which was our best side or if our hair looked best up or down. We also did quite a lot of gloating to girls in other classes, talking in loud voices about film crews and camera angles and so on. Although the older girls pretended they thought it was all kids' stuff, we knew they were very jealous that it wasn't *their* class.

As luck would have it, we had history as our last lesson – history in our own classroom with Mrs Mackie. We were all absolutely jumpy with excitement by this time, especially when Philippa made up some desperate story about having to go to the loo and reported back in a loud whisper that there were two huge green vans outside. The film unit had arrived!

Mrs Mackie was making a brave attempt to

talk about the second world war but no one was really listening to her. We were all writing notes to each other saying what we were going to do in front of the cameras and Cerise and Jane were gossiping loudly.

'Enough!' Mrs Mackie said. 'Stop talking, Jane!'

'I was just telling Cerise what I'm going to say about Park Wood,' Jane said, smiling sweetly.

'Indeed?' Mrs Mackie said. 'Well, you won't be *at* Park Wood much longer unless you do some work!' she said. 'I will not have my classes constantly disrupted by you and your antics.'

Jasbir put her hand up. 'It *is* a bit exciting, though, isn't it, Mrs Mackie?' she said, 'what with the TV people coming and everything.'

'No it isn't, Arina – I mean Jasbir,' Mrs Mackie said, irritated. 'I am not concerned with cheap . . .'

But just then the door opened and Miss Harmer swept in accompanied by two men with bits of cameras hung all over them and four other people.

There was a sort of collective squeal of excitement and we all jiggled in our seats impatiently, patted our hair and straightened our jumpers. Cerise got out a mirror and put on some cerise lipstick.

'Ah, Mrs Mackie!' Miss Harmer said. She was wearing a revolting yellowy tweed suit. 'I've told these two TV chaps that you wouldn't mind a bit if they started before your class has finished. They're anxious to get the natural light before it fades, I believe.'

'Well, I don't know about that. . .' Mrs Mackie spluttered.

'Come now, Mrs Mackie, this is an exciting day for Park Wood,' Miss Harmer said as we all threw our books back in our desks. 'I'm sure that you are as concerned as I am that the school and the girls are seen at their absolute best. What's half an hour of history compared to that?'

'Oh, very little, Miss Harmer,' said Mrs Mackie sarcastically, 'very little indeed. Half an hour of the Great War – why that's only a few hundred people killed, slain on . . .'

'Thank *you*, Mrs Mackie!' Miss Harmer said. She looked round the class. 'Well, I'm pleased to see that you've followed my directive on improving your classroom. I should think so, too!'

Fleur and I held our breath – it was a touch and go moment – but Mrs Mackie was so insensed by the film crew as more and more of them poured into the room, that she couldn't have registered what Miss Harmer was saying.

Jane glided out to the front and spoke carelessly to the men with cameras. 'Hi, Jeff . . . Bill,' she said. 'Find the old place all right? Is Loretta with you? I desperately want her to do something with my cheekbones.'

Mrs Mackie looked at the scene in front of

her, tutted very loudly and very long, and then, studiously ignoring everyone else, began writing up something in one of her note books. Men wheeled in great arc lights, rolls of rubbery cable were fed through windows, microphones were dotted about, cameras were trundled through doorways knocking paintwork off ('Don't worry about that!' Miss Harmer said, 'doesn't matter a bit!') and through it all Mrs Mackie just sat, writing away.

The room was filled with lights, cameras, women with clipboards and men with stopwatches. It didn't look like our classroom at all – apart from Mrs Mackie sitting out the front.

We sat there in the middle of everything, marooned on our desks and scared to move off in case we got shouted at. I'd stepped down once, but I'd nearly got run over by a great trolley thing and had just thrown myself back on to my desk in the nick of time.

Miss Harmer was striding about, getting in everyone's way and telling those who didn't know and couldn't care less who she was: 'I'm Doris Harmer, school headmistress, pleased to meet you,' I heard her say at least thirty times.

The man called Jeff clapped his hands. 'We'll have a few trial shots,' he said. 'And we'll start with Ara sitting at her desk and the rest of you girls milling around her ... as if she's telling you something.'

Well, we didn't need asking twice – we all

jumped up and bolted over to where 'Ara' was.

'Out of my way!' I heard Alison say, and she jabbed her elbow in Mouse's ribs and doubled her up. Jasbir pulled Arina out of the way, there were screams as girls trod on other girls' feet, but by scrambling and scuffling I managed to get myself right next to Jane, my face just centimetres away from hers.

Jeff laughed. 'You're all supposed to be listening to her, not eating her,' he said. 'Just back off a bit, will you?'

We all regretfully backed off and he and two of the women grouped us how they wanted us. ('Ooh, me! Me! I'm her best friend!' Cerise squealed, and got herself at the front).

Mrs Mackie reminded us she was still there by slamming her drawer shut. 'School's finished. Time to go,' she said. 'Goodnight girls. Perhaps in the morning we can continue with some proper school work. Today it's been like a bear garden.'

'Oh – you're not going!' one of the women with clipboards said. 'We want you in the film.'

'Well, I'm afraid you'll have to want on,' Mrs Mackie said crisply, moving towards the door.

'Oh please!' Jeff said, turning on his heel. 'We must have one of Ara with her teacher! A photograph to convey some of the friendly two-way dialogue between the young girl actress and her mentor!'

'Ridiculous!' Mrs Mackie said, hand on the doorknob.

'I want our viewers to see how important a steady, disciplined school life is to a young actress . . .' he said wheedlingly.

'Do you indeed!' Mrs Mackie said, suddenly showing a spark of interest. 'My sentiments entirely.'

Jeff moved quickly and, putting a hand under her elbow, propelled her smoothly towards Jane's desk, talking all the while. 'So if you could just . . . the viewers will be fascinated . . . teachers all over the country will be absolutely engrossed . . .'

'I really don't know that . . .' Mrs Mackie said, allowing herself to be sat down next to Jane.

There was a slight cough from the front of the class and when we looked Miss Harmer was squinting her thin and horrible smile at Jeff.

'Ah yes . . . how could we forget the importance of the head teacher in acting as a flagship for the rest of the school,' Jeff said smoothly. 'Perhaps you, Miss Harmer, would like to come and sit on the other side of Araminta and then both you and Mrs Mackie can each look at her – just as if you're giving her some of your invaluable advice.'

Mrs Mackie began bristling a bit at having Miss Harmer so near and I think she might have got up again, but Bill rushed up. 'Wonderful shot!' he said. 'Anyone can see what rapport you teachers have got with the young.'

Sniggers of laughter shot round the class at this but Jeff shouted above all the din, 'Can we have a run through with a voice over, please!'

A girl rushed up with a clapperboard. 'Araminta Eversage: A day in the life, Take one!' she shouted, and then someone else started reading a script . . .

'Araminta Eversage is young and talented, but of course she needs to keep her feet firmly on the ground, and that's why her parents chose to send her to an ordinary school.

'At Park Wood Girls' School, Araminta can mix with a wide cross-section of girls, and is helped to keep a steady outlook on life by her class teacher, Mrs Mackie, and her head teacher, Miss Harmer . . .'

'Could you look first at one teacher, then the other,' Bill instructed Jane. 'And Mrs Mackie – can you pat Ara's hand and give her a lovely smile, please.'

Well, only we all knew what a supreme effort it cost Mrs Mackie to smile and pat Jane's hand, but she managed it. When we talked about it afterwards we all reckoned that she deserved an Oscar.

'Wonderful, darling!' Bill said, giving Mrs Mackie a hug when she'd done her bit. 'You're a natural!'

Well, her face! It was so outraged that we all – the whole class – exploded with laughter and the giggles lasted us through all the rest of the filming – which consisted mostly of Jane swanning around the classroom bestowing smiles on us, pausing briefly by our desks to say a few words of wisdom and generally playing the part of Most Popular Girl in the School. When the film was shown on television in the Easter holidays we were to be seen slightly out of focus in the background either clutching our sides, stuffing our hands over our mouths or bursting out into fresh fits of hysterics.

All in all it had been a pretty good term – and I didn't think I'd done quite as many daft things, either. Course, the skiing trip would be another story . . .

Read more about Mickey, Cerise, Fleur, Araminta and the other first year girls at Park Wood Girls' School in:

School Friends 3: *Park Wood on Ice*

'The trip to the French alps turned out to be really exciting, what with the mystery of Mrs Mackie's disappearing underwear, Cerise getting stupid over the skiing instructor, the dormitory ghost, the fancy dress midnight feast and the strike over the revolting food. We even managed to get in quite a bit of skiing!'